THE BEACH BABY

A SUNNY ISLE OF PALMS NOVEL (BOOK 1)

GRACE PALMER

JOIN MY MAILING LIST!

Click the link below to join my mailing list and receive updates, freebies, release announcements, and more!

JOIN HERE:

https://sendfox.com/lp/19y8p3

ALSO BY GRACE PALMER
A SUNNY ISLE OF PALMS NOVEL (BOOK 1)

THE BEACH BABY

Charlene Wilson is in over her head.

Isle of Palms is supposed to be her little slice of paradise—and for a while, it was. She and her husband, Davy, had a successful house flipping business, a happy family, a bright future.

Then it all changed.

Davy passed away too soon and left her with massive medical bills.

The house Charlene is trying to flip can't find any buyers and she's running out of money.

And her troubled daughter hasn't been seen in more than five years.

Add to that her younger sister coming back to the Isle of Palms unexpectedly for the first time in a decade, and Charlene is feeling more overwhelmed than ever.

She uses her 45th birthday wish to hope that, just once, things will end up okay.

Then she walks outside...

And finds a baby on her doorstep.

There's a note, too. It says,

Dear Mom: His name is Tyler.

I can't keep him.

Look after him for me.

And suddenly, all of Charlene's other problems don't seem so important after all.

1

LATE SUMMER—JUST BEFORE DAWN —ISLE OF PALMS, SOUTH CAROLINA

Charlene Wilson stood alone on the beach, watching as the sun came up on her forty-fifth birthday.

She knew there would be a bouquet of white peonies waiting on her doorstep when she got home. Before her husband Davy died, he'd made arrangements with a local florist to keep the deliveries coming every year.

She knew with just as much certainty that there would be nothing from her daughter. The days of Margaret sending hand-drawn birthday cards were long gone. The days of Margaret talking to her at all were also gone.

Other things would be waiting, too. A leak in the upstairs sink she needed to fix. A wonky curtain rod over one of the windows facing the backyard.

And, hopefully, a pair of buyers who would write her a check for this godforsaken house and let her turn her back on it forever.

It shouldn't be too hard to sell. I've done it plenty of times before, Charlene thought. As a house flipper, selling houses was her job. This one felt different, though. Because it was *their* house. The one she and Davy had bought to fix up for themselves. The one they'd hoped to grow old in.

She was growing old in it, for sure. But Davy wasn't. Neither was their daughter. And even if Charlene could afford to keep the house—which she very much couldn't—she had no desire to grow old in it alone.

The sky overhead was cotton candy pink and sherbet orange. The beach was empty of other people at this hour, but the animals were all awake and busy. Seagulls swooped down to fetch breakfast from the waters. Fish speckled the glassy surface. Ghost crabs skittered through the beach grasses behind her.

Charlene had already checked to be sure all the turtle nests remained undisturbed. They would be born any day now. She hoped to be here to see the precious baby turtles emerge from the dunes and scurry down to the ocean. Nothing else in her life felt quite so pure or so wholesome.

"Happy birthday to Charleeeeeneeee," a familiar voice crooned in the distance.

Charlene turned and saw Elaine picking her way down between sand dunes, two paper coffee cups in her hands. The older woman kept her eyes on her feet, but she wore an incandescent smile.

"For the lovely Charlene Wilson," Elaine said when she was closer, holding out a coffee cup. "Happiest of birthdays, honey."

"You shouldn't have," Charlene said as she grabbed the cup and took a grateful sip. It was more sugar and cream than it was coffee. But then again, it was her birthday, so maybe she deserved something sweet.

"And why shouldn't I?"

"Because it's unnecessary," Charlene said. "Seeing you on my morning walks is treat enough."

Elaine chuckled. "If I stopped doing things just because they were unnecessary, I'd have to quit doing all of my favorite things. A good bottle of red wine is wholly unnecessary and yet you'll have to pry the stuff out of my cold, dead hands."

"Red wine has antioxidants, I think. But otherwise, point taken."

"Besides," Elaine continued with a wry grin, "showering you with love on your birthday is completely necessary. I've been doing it for the last fifteen years and I see no reason to stop now."

Fifteen years. The idea seemed impossible, but sure enough, it was fifteen years to the day that Charlene had met Elaine. At an ice cream shop of all places.

Charlene had gone into Ye Old Fashioned over in Mount Pleasant— which served the best banana split in the Lowcountry—to pick up a birthday cake for herself on a whim. When Elaine overheard Charlene's conversation with the cashier, she'd butted in.

"No one is buying their own birthday cake on my watch!" Elaine had announced, checkbook in hand. "How much?"

Charlene had invited Elaine to have a glass of wine on the porch later that night in repayment. They'd been fast friends ever since.

Elaine took a loud sip of her coffee and kicked her sandals off, pressing her toes into the damp sand. "No one should buy their own birthday cake or make their own coffee on their birthday. It's that simple."

"I don't think this is an argument I can win, so I'll just say, 'Thank you.'"

"Smart woman." Elaine's brown eyes glimmered. "So, any other birthday plans today?"

Charlene shook her head. There was no sense in lying. "Not really."

Elaine *tsked* her disapproval. "I've had almost twice as many birthdays as you and I still insist on celebrating each and every one of them."

"I think you might be fudging the math there a bit," Charlene chuckled. "But honestly, I've just never been big on birthdays."

"Pish-posh, bah humbug," Elaine teased. "Perhaps this is my only child syndrome speaking out. You folks with siblings are always much better at sharing the spotlight. Speaking of which, will you see your sister today? I haven't spoken to Annette in... gosh, it's been a long time."

That makes two of us, Charlene thought privately.

Out loud, she said, "Maybe."

"What about Margaret?" Elaine asked. "How is she doing?"

This was not the conversation she wanted to be having on her birthday. Charlene bit back a sigh and smiled the way parents were supposed to smile when asked about their children.

"Fine. She's busy. Still living in New York City."

Or is she? she thought bitterly. Really, it was anyone's guess where Margaret was. But this way was easier than explaining the whole ugly truth.

"I hope you talk to her, at least," Elaine said. "I worry about you being all alone in that old house. Davy wouldn't like it."

"Well, you won't have to worry about me being in that house alone for much longer. I have buyers coming to look at it today."

Elaine gasped. "It's on the market?"

"Not yet," Charlene said. "But my go-to realtor, Jamie, has a young couple looking to buy something big and beachfront. She thought of me first and called to ask if I was ready to show."

"And you are? Last I heard, you were in the middle of rebuilding the back patio and painting every room in the house."

"That was two months ago!" Charlene countered. "Two months in the house-flipping business is a year in the normal world. I've got the place all spruced up. Just have to take down all my personal stuff off the walls. As soon as that's done, I'm all set."

She hoped she was all set, at least. She didn't have any more money to pour into the house. It was hard to afford painters and plumbers and carpenters when she was still paying off the remaining overdue bills for hospital visits, experimental treatments, and Davy's in-home nurse. It was a miracle the money had stretched as far as it had. It wouldn't stretch much farther.

"That's exciting," Elaine said. "I'll have to come see it before some lucky person snatches it up."

"The couple coming today is moving from Oklahoma. I'm hoping the ocean view alone will be enough to seal the deal."

"Not many oceanfront properties in the Great Plains, I suppose."

And if that still wasn't enough, Isle of Palms would do the rest of the selling for her. Who could say no to warm sun year-round, palm trees draping the main boulevard, and all the delicious seafood restaurants clustered together on Front Beach? Charlene always told people this place was a little slice of heaven. She meant it.

"It's as good as done, then. You've never had a problem flipping properties before. Why would this one be any different?" Elaine asked.

That same thought had been running through Charlene's head for days. Yes, this one mattered more than all the others that had come before it. But only to her. Only she knew how tough things had gotten.

To everyone else, it was just another beautiful home on a beautiful island.

Charlene nodded. "You're right. I'm sure it will all work out."

"Where are you going to live if it sells?" Elaine asked. "What about our morning beach walks?"

"I'll pay off debts and then use the leftover money to get a condo in Wild Dunes. Still within walking distance."

"Good. I'd miss seeing that smile of yours every morning."

Charlene smiled. "Right back at you, Elaine."

Her morning walk was her daily meditation. And meeting up with Elaine halfway was a fun bonus. Some days, Elaine was the only living soul that Charlene spoke to, and Charlene didn't want to give that up. She'd learned the hard way since... well, since everything that had happened, to hold tight to what little she had left.

Once the sun was fully over the horizon and the humidity started to make itself known, Elaine and Charlene parted ways with a final "Happy Birthday" hug.

"Today will work out, okay?" Elaine whispered in Charlene's ear. "Everything is going to be fine."

"I know," Charlene whispered right back.

But she didn't know. She didn't know anything at all.

∾

On her way back home, the realtor called.

"Hey, Jamie," Charlene answered.

"Today is the day!" Jamie responded, chipper as always despite the hour. "I just wanted to call and let you know their flight should be in at eight this morning, but I doubt we'll be at your house before nine. Does that work?"

"Sounds great. I only have a few last-minute things to take care of. Putting pictures away, turning on the diffuser. That kind of jazz."

"Oh, the lemongrass?" Jamie asked. "I stole that trick from you, y'know? I use it at every single one of my open houses now. People love it."

Charlene laughed. "That's the one. I hope they'll love it. And the rest of the house, too."

"You've done a great job with the place. They'll be tripping all over themselves to get the keys," she insisted. "Anyhoo, see you there in a bit!"

Charlene hoped Jamie was right. As she stepped off the beach access path and crossed her own tidy lawn, she couldn't see any reason anyone would want to pass on the house. After all her hard work, it was perfect.

It hadn't always been perfect, though. "The point isn't to live in a perfect house. The point is to be happy, right?" Davy had said when they'd bought the place a decade earlier. "It's fine if it takes us twenty years to finish the renovations around here. We've got the time."

He was wrong about that, though. They didn't have the time.

They'd done some things over the years, whenever they could find a spare hour here or there. They'd managed to repaint the "puke green siding," as Margaret had so eloquently put it, to a crisp white. To tear out the ancient carpets in favor of the original hardwood hidden beneath.

Charlene shoved thoughts of the past aside and went up the stairs. The coffee Elaine had bought her had provided more of a sugar-high than a caffeine kick. Best to get to work immediately before she crashed back down to earth.

She went to open the door, but to her surprise, it was locked. That was strange. Isle of Palms was such a safe, friendly place that she thought nothing of stepping out with the door unlocked behind her. Maybe old age forgetfulness was creeping up on her faster than she realized.

Charlene fished the key from her pocket, unlocked the door, and stepped into the house.

As she closed the door behind her, there was a thudding sound at the other end of the breezeway. She looked around. The curtain covering the paned window in the center of the door rustled like someone had just moved past it.

For a moment, she froze, listening to the house around her. Waiting for the telltale sound of creaking floorboards or the metallic *ting* of a murderer's knife being slid from a sheath.

But there was nothing. Charlene was alone.

"You silly old goose," she mumbled to herself. "Losing it already?"

Charlene shrugged and did her walkthrough of the house. As she went, she took down the personal photos from the walls. She did her best not to look at them too closely. She was afraid what would happen if she caught a glimpse of Margaret, freckle-faced and innocent at eleven. Or Davy, suited up and beaming on their wedding day. To say nothing of anything involving her and Annette. The last thing she wanted was to be a blubbering, teary mess when the buyers arrived.

Everything else was ship-shape. All three of the upstairs bedrooms looked spacious, tidy, inviting. The study glowed with morning sun. A salty breeze rippled through the screened-in back porch.

The only issue, Charlene noticed with annoyance, was that the faucet in the upstairs bathroom was leaking again. Just a drip. But a noticeable drip.

"Easy fix," the discount plumber had claimed last week when he was done looking at it. "Won't ever bother you again."

"So much for an easy fix," Charlene muttered. She made a mental note to find a new plumber as she shook the taps, hoping to stop the dripping. When that didn't work, she stuffed the photos she'd gathered into a spare cardboard box and then headed downstairs to get her wrench.

All she needed was for the drip to stop long enough for the buyers to see the house. Then she'd call another plumber and have it properly sorted after they left.

She found her toolbox under the sink, plucked out a wrench, and turned to go back upstairs. But the moment Charlene set foot on the staircase, there was a knock on the front door.

She checked her watch with a frown. It was a hair past eight. There was no way the buyers were here this early, right? It couldn't be. But just in case, she strapped on her brightest smile and pulled the door open to greet whoever it might be.

It wasn't the buyers, though. Not by a long shot.

Instead, standing on her porch was a little boy. He was probably three, definitely no older than four.

And she had no clue who he was—until he looked up at her with huge, soulful eyes and said, "Hi, Grandma."

2

EARLY MORNING AT CHARLENE WILSON'S HOUSE

The little boy was standing next to a ratty suitcase and a beat-up car seat. He blinked up at Charlene expectantly. A chill ran through her body—those wide green eyes were so spookily familiar.

She leaned through her front door and looked around, expecting to see another adult. Someone, anyone, who could explain who this poor child was and why he seemed to think Charlene was his grandmother.

But as she did, he held out his hand. In it, there was a note.

"Is this for me?" she asked him.

He didn't respond. She took the paper and unfolded it.

His name is Tyler. I can't keep him. Look after him for me.

Charlene's heart froze at the sight of the familiar messy scrawl.

How many boxes of schoolwork and letters to Santa did she have stashed away in the attic with this exact writing on it?

Maybe Charlene didn't know where her daughter lived or what she was doing, but she could still recognize her handwriting. No matter how many years had passed.

This note was from Margaret. This note was proof Margaret was *alive*.

Given the lifestyle she led, the choices she made, there were no guarantees of that. But now, here she was. Some form of her, at least. A short note with no explanation left in the tiny hands of a tiny boy.

"Did your mommy give this to you?" Charlene asked. Some part of her hoped the boy would shake his head. Tell her some bizarre story that would make this make sense.

Instead, the little boy shrunk down between his shoulders like a turtle, but nodded.

Charlene sighed. She read the note again. ***His name is Tyler. I can't keep him. Look after him for me.***

Five years without a phone call. Or a letter. Or a text message. And now… this.

A child.

A *grandson*.

Charlene knelt down to the little boy's level. "Tyler? Is that your name?"

He was too shy to even nod now. This close, Charlene could see his eyes were actually hazel—green with streaks of brown and gold. She'd seen them before in another little face, many years ago. She ignored the gut punch of recognition.

"Did your mommy leave you here, Tyler?"

He trembled like a leaf.

"It's okay, honey," she said.

His chin dimpled with a pout. His cheeks turned a splotchy red.

"No, no. Don't cry. It's okay," Charlene pleaded.

A second later, the little boy—Tyler, according to Margaret's note; she repeated in her head a dozen times as if tasting it, *TylerTylerTylerTylerTyler*—scrunched up his face and began to cry.

Charlene stood up and pressed her fingers into her temple. She'd never been good with kids.

"It's different with your own children," Charlene's mom had told her when she was pregnant with Margaret. *"The bond you have with your own child is stronger than anything in the world. There's no reason to worry."*

Wrong on at least one count. Over the years, Charlene had found plenty of reasons to worry.

Margaret had been a daddy's girl from the start. When she was crying or hurt or angry, she wouldn't calm down until Charlene handed her to Davy. It continued that way through skinned knees, through first pimples, through rumors spread by mean girls at school. Davy could fix anything.

Until the doctors gave Davy one year to live.

No one could fix that. Not even the doctors.

"Stop pretending you care!" Margaret had screeched at Charlene after the guests and mourners had emptied out of the wake, leaving behind a lifetime's worth of leftover cheesy potatoes and fruit trays.

"Of course I care. I'm your mom."

"When has that ever meant anything?" Margaret had eyeliner smeared around her eyes, but the rest of her face was bare. Without her usual armor of foundation and angry streaks of blush, she looked years younger. "Dad was the only one who even liked me."

"That's not true, Mar," Charlene argued. "You know that's not true."

"Don't tell me what I know."

Charlene had taken a breath and tried to channel the calm Davy was able to come by so naturally. "I miss him, too. It's going to be hard without him, but we can—"

"Get through this together?" Margaret had finished. She barked out a humorless laugh. "Please. Dad would have gotten through it himself if it hadn't been for you."

"What is that supposed to mean?"

"It means you cared more about saving a few dollars than saving him," Margaret snapped.

There weren't any dollars to save. They'd spent it all. Taken out lines of credit. Sold whatever they could to give Davy the best chance.

But Charlene couldn't tell her daughter that. Couldn't admit there was nothing left.

"There were still more treatments to try. More doctors to see. But you gave up on him!"

Her daughter was wrong about that. It had been Davy's call to stop the treatments. He wanted to come back to the house and spend his final weeks in his own bed, free of IVs and beeping machines and brisk, humorless nurses.

"We can talk about this later when we're both calm." Charlene knew Margaret needed time and space. But as Charlene had pulled Margaret's bedroom door closed behind her, she'd had no idea exactly how much time and space her daughter needed.

The answer was five years' worth, apparently.

No note, no explanation, no goodbye. All Margaret had left behind was Charlene's wallet laying on the kitchen counter, all the cash inside stolen away.

"And now this is how she repays me." The boy's shrill crying was already giving Charlene a headache. She had no idea how to make it stop. She dragged a hand down her face in dismay.

Then she heard tires coming down the driveway.

Charlene snapped her head up with horror. Sure enough, Jamie's white SUV was trundling up Charlene's driveway. She could make out two blurry figures in the backseat.

The buyers.

"No," she hissed. "No, no, *NO!*"

Tyler started to cry harder.

"Oh, no, I wasn't talking to you, sweetie," Charlene stammered. She hurried him inside the house with a firm hand on his back. "You're fine. You're not in trouble."

He tipped his head back, fat tears rolling down his cheeks.

"Do you want a snack? Or a drink? I have—" *Water, coffee, and wine.* Nothing else. Dairy had started giving her trouble once she got north of forty, so she didn't even have milk in the fridge.

"Oh, TV!" Charlene said. She bent down to scoop Tyler up and rested him on her hip as she started to head towards the living room. When his cries reached a new, ear-splitting decibel, she changed course and headed upstairs. "What do you like to watch? I have basic cable."

As if the boy would know what that meant.

She opened the guest room with her hip and planted Tyler on the end of the bed. She dug through three dresser drawers before she found the remote. The local news popped up first, the anchor talking about an armed robbery that happened overnight. Charlene flipped through the stations until she found a kid's show. A cartoon tiger wearing a red cardigan. It looked safe enough.

"Do you like this show?"

Tyler couldn't even hear her over his own crying. Things seemed to get worse every time Charlene opened her mouth. She turned the volume up on the TV and left, shutting the door behind her.

"This is fine," she said to herself. Sweat was collecting between her shoulder blades. She felt faint. "The buyers are here. Tyler has the television on. They don't even need to see that room."

Davy had always made fun of her for talking to herself when she was stressed. But Charlene couldn't think about Davy right now. Or Margaret. Or the fact that her daughter was probably flying away down the highway right now, putting untold miles between herself and this problem.

Charlene needed to focus on the buyers. Just for the next half hour. Then, she'd… figure something out with Tyler.

She just needed to get through the next half hour.

"… The bricks are original, though Charlene gave them a white wash when she replaced boards on the porch and put in the new railing," Jamie was saying when Charlene stepped onto the front porch.

The buyers were a young couple, barely thirty. The man wore a dark blue suit and a furrowed brow. His wife, a pretty picture in a gauzy white dress and leather sandals, smiled as she admired the yard.

"It's beautiful. Isn't it beautiful, Chris?" she sighed.

"We'd have to hire a lawn service for the garden beds," Chris remarked.

Charlene cleared her throat and waved. "There's actually landscape fabric underneath those beds. It was recommended to me by a professional landscaper years ago. It makes upkeep super easy."

"Oh, here she is," Jamie said. "Chris, Katie, this is Charlene. And this is exactly why she's here. Usually, I send owners away for the walkthrough, but Charlene is a house-flipper. She'll be able to answer all of your questions."

"You also lived here, right?" Chris asked.

"For ten years," Charlene answered. "But don't worry, I'll try to be impartial."

They laughed and Jamie carried on pointing out the new windows, the freshly-painted black shutters, and the deep, shaded porch where Charlene and Davy used to drink sweet tea on warm summer afternoons.

Chris scrutinized everything with a careful eye as they moved to head inside. Katie, on the other hand, seemed bewitched. "It's all so magical. Like I'm on a movie set," she murmured. "It's too beautiful to be real."

"The whole island makes me feel like that," Charlene said. "But trust me, it's all real. It's a great area to raise kids. So much room for them to play."

Jamie stepped forward. "But it's also quiet. Secluded."

"Absolutely. Best of both worlds." Charlene reached for the front door.

As soon as she pulled it open, crying filled the air. Katie's smile slipped and Chris's frown deepened. Jamie looked at Charlene with an unspoken question written all over her face. *Since when do you have a kid?*

"Oh no! Sounds like someone is upset," Katie said.

Charlene tried to smile. "Yeah, that's just… Tyler." *My grandson.* The words felt clunky even in her brain. Charlene couldn't imagine saying them out loud.

"Your son?" Katie asked.

"No, no. Not mine. Not my son. He's…"

My daughter's son. But that felt complicated. Charlene wanted to make it out of this situation without ever having to explain a word of it to Jamie. Jamie didn't even know about Margaret. And whose business was it, anyway?

"He's someone else's son."

The crying seemed to be growing louder. Watching TV was supposed to turn children into zombies. *The digital pacifier,* Davy always called it. Why oh why wasn't it working now, today of all days?

Charlene clenched her fists so tight the knuckles on her right hand popped. She smiled. "I'm babysitting. Last minute thing. I'm really sorry."

"Don't be sorry," Katie said. "I'm a preschool teacher, so believe me, I know how it goes. Kids can be a handful."

"Whose son is he? Do I know them?" Jamie asked.

"Oh, um..." Charlene fumbled for a believable explanation. Naming a real person had obvious risks. Making a name up had risks, too. The last thing she wanted was to get caught in a lie. "No, you don't know them. Just a friend. An old friend."

Everyone was staring at her. Their eyes were like lasers. Charlene felt hot.

Katie looked up the stairs towards the sound of the shrieking. "If you need to go check on him, then—"

"No, he'll be okay. Don't worry about him. He does this all the time. I'll show you around."

"Luckily, the screaming child isn't a permanent fixture in the house," Jamie teased. She gritted her teeth in what was supposed to be a smile. It looked more like a grimace. A crying baby wasn't exactly catnip to house buyers. She was probably wishing she'd told Charlene to clear out after all.

"Even if he was, I'd have to consider it," Katie said. She walked into the breezeway, head tipped back to admire the crown molding around the ceiling. "Goodness gracious, it's so beautiful."

Chris pointed to the stairs. "Is the banister solid wood?"

"Oak. Just installed last month. The old was held together with glue and prayers," Charlene joked. "This one matches the original as closely as possible."

It was easier to talk about the house. Even with the crying still floating down the stairs, Charlene felt like she was treading water. She could make it through this. Just a few more minutes.

She took a step backward to let Chris and Katie admire the woodwork—but instantly, her sandal was wet.

"What on earth…" Charlene muttered. She was standing in a puddle at the base of the stairs.

As if on cue, the crying form upstairs stopped. Cut off like someone had simply pulled the plug. That's when Charlene heard it: the sound of dripping water.

Katie gasped. "Oh no!" She nudged Chris and pointed at the stairs. He winced.

Water was dripping down the stairs in a thin, steady stream. *Plop. Plop. Plop.* From one stair down to the next, a dozen little waterfalls in miniature.

"Did the kiddo flood the bathroom?" Jamie asked. She turned to Chris and Katie. "My son once shoved an entire basket of hand towels into our toilet and flushed. What a bill that was."

Charlene moved up the stairs, careful not to slip. But when she stopped in front of the bathroom door, falling suddenly didn't seem like such a bad option. A tumble down the stairs would have at least put her out of her misery.

In good news, the leak from the faucet tap had finally stopped. In devastatingly bad news, water was now gushing out from the pipes beneath the sink. The bathroom and hallway were flooded an inch deep.

"Everything okay up there?" Chris called.

"Oh, yeah, totally. It's... I can handle it." Charlene tried to work out the logistics of running downstairs to turn off the water without Jamie, Chris, or Katie noticing. The odds weren't in her favor.

Then she felt a tug on the back of her pants.

Charlene turned to see Tyler standing at her feet. His socks were soaked through and his eyes were red and puffy. "Grandma, I have to potty."

"Grandma?" Katie whispered the word, but it carried.

Charlene squeezed her eyes closed. By the time she turned off the water and got Tyler on the toilet, Katie and Chris were already outside.

"They have another showing a few blocks up the road," Jamie explained. "They don't want to be late."

Charlene's heart dropped. "I'll have this mess cleaned up in just a few minutes if they want to come back. Nothing some towels and an emergency call to a plumber can't fix, right?"

"I'm sorry, Charlene," Jamie whispered, "but I think they're out. It was just... an off day."

Tears burned the back of her eyes. Charlene cleared her throat and nodded. "Yeah, sure. The house isn't even listed yet. It will be fine."

Jamie patted her on the shoulder. "We'll get the next one. Don't worry."

Don't worry. Calm down. Relax. A list of phrases Charlene had heard her entire life that had never once made her feel any better. How could you tell a drowning person not to worry about the water in their lungs?

Still, Charlene smiled and waved as Jamie walked across the porch and down to the car. It was already idling in the driveway.

Charlene could hear Tyler's tiny footsteps splashing through the water upstairs. She knew she needed to find towels and start cleaning up the mess. She needed to call a real plumber and beg him to come help her. She needed to get her house on the market as soon as possible before the bank could get antsy about her latest missed payment. She needed to figure out how to get in touch with Margaret and what she was going to do about Tyler.

Instead of doing all or any of that, though, Charlene just leaned against her front door and sunk down to the floor. Her knees folded into her chest.

Happy birthday to me, she thought.

Then she started to cry.

3

MID-MORNING AT DEPARTMENT OF SOCIAL SERVICES OFFICE

The doors of the Charleston County Department of Social Services were like mirrors. Charlene couldn't see anything inside, but she could see herself standing on the sidewalk. Tyler's left hand was in hers. His other hand rubbed at his tired eyes.

The drive to DSS had taken forty-two minutes. Tyler cried for thirty-five of them. Charlene was half-inclined to join him.

The boy had already been abandoned once today. Could Charlene bring herself to make it twice?

This was different, though. She wasn't abandoning him on some doorstep with a lousy note. She was taking care of him. Freeing him from the cycle of bad parenting that had led to all of this in the first place. If Charlene hadn't figured out how to raise Margaret, how was she supposed to raise Tyler?

This case was exactly the kind of situation DSS was supposed to handle. They'd help Tyler. Things would be better for him.

So why couldn't she open the door?

Suddenly, a man in a dirt-stained work shirt walked outside, a phone pressed to his ear. "... No, they won't tell me anything. I've been waiting for an hour, but when I got to the front of the line, they just—"

He stuttered to a stop a few inches in front of Charlene. "Oh, sorry." He turned around to grab the door before it could close and held it open for her.

Instinct alone propelled Charlene forward. She thanked him, but the words were lost in the cacophony coming from the DSS lobby. Apparently, the front doors were soundproof, too.

Crying and ringing telephones overwhelmed her senses. On top of it all, everyone in the room was talking loudly to be heard over the chaos. It was a solid wall of sound. Tyler tucked himself closer to Charlene's leg.

"We'll go sit over there and wait for it to calm down," she said, pulling on his hand.

"You'll be waiting forever if you do that."

Charlene turned and saw a tall man with salt and pepper hair standing against a bulletin board. Pictures of missing children and flyers promoting outdated donation drives hung around him.

"Excuse me?" she asked.

"It won't calm down," he explained. "It never does. You'd be better off going home and calling for an appointment."

"The website said walk-ins were welcome." Charlene had admittedly only scanned the website for a minute or two, but she was positive she'd read that somewhere.

He nodded. "And you are. Welcome, that is. Welcome to wait until close of day and then come back tomorrow to try again."

Tomorrow? No, Charlene needed to talk to someone *today*. Immediately. She couldn't take Tyler home with her.

"I think I'll take my chances, thanks."

She was about to turn away from the man when Tyler pulled on her pinky finger. "I need to go potty."

"You just went before we left the house."

He squirmed in place, his feet pedaling against the floor.

"The bathroom off the lobby is being renovated. You'll have to use the one next door at the food distribution center," the man said.

"Thanks," Charlene deadpanned. She started moving towards the door, but the man stepped forward, cutting off her path.

"And if you have to get out of line, don't expect anyone to save your spot. It's ruthless around here."

"Noted."

Before he could say anything else, Charlene tugged Tyler away and to the building next door.

When they got back ten minutes later, the line stretching out from the lone available clerk had doubled.

"No," she groaned.

"Yes," a now familiar male voice said.

Charlene fought an eye roll. The man with salt and pepper hair was no longer standing in front of the bulletin board, but had moved to the opposite side of the entryway. He was sitting in a padded chair, his ankle resting on the opposite knee.

He smiled and gave her a small wave. "I'm telling you, just call tomorrow. Waiting here is pointless."

"And who are you exactly?"

The man leaned forward, hand extended. "Noah."

Charlene considered not taking it, but politeness won out. She shook his hand. "Charlene."

"Pleasure." There was a lilt to his voice that Charlene couldn't interpret. Was he mocking her?

She knew how it looked, showing up to DSS with a little boy, desperate to talk to someone. A thousand different unflattering assumption could be made about her. But this rude man didn't know her situation. Who was he to judge?

Charlene pulled her hand back and wiped it on her pant leg. "Thanks for the advice, but I'll take my chances."

As she walked away, she could hear him mumble to himself, "Don't say I didn't warn you."

Tyler was surprisingly quiet for a three-year-old. He waited patiently next to Charlene, looking around as they inched their way towards the front of the line.

"Do you want a snack?" She handed him the chocolate chip granola bar she kept in her purse for emergencies. He studied it suspiciously for only a second before taking a big bite right out of her hand.

Charlene could remember taking Margaret to the mall when she was about Tyler's age. They'd only been there for five minutes when Margaret spotted the ice cream shop in the food court. Another five minutes later, Charlene was carrying Margaret, kicking and screaming, out of the mall under her arm.

"I would have bought her an ice cream cone," Charlene's sister, Annette, had said under her breath. "We didn't have to leave."

Charlene shook her head. "It's the principle. I told her 'no' and that means 'no.' She has to learn."

"This is why I'll never have children," Annette had teased.

True to her word, Annette never did.

Instead, she and her husband, Frederick, funneled all the money they would have spent on children into trips to the Italian Riviera and Paris. Charlene hadn't received a vacation postcard from them in years, but she assumed they were still traveling somewhere.

Globetrotting vacations aside, it was hard for Charlene not to envy Annette sometimes. She could never regret having Margaret, of course, no matter what had happened between them.

But the idea of no sleep regressions to zombie walk their way through... No temper tantrums to manage... No grandchildren abandoned on her front porch...

A simpler life it would be, indeed.

When Tyler finished his snack, he handed Charlene the wrapper to throw away. There was a trash can along the far wall, but Charlene caught sight of the dark-haired man still sitting in the front lobby. His warning rang in her ears.

And if you have to get out of line again, don't expect anyone to save your spot. It's ruthless around here.

She shoved the trash in her back pocket and stayed put in the motionless line.

As they inched closer to the front desk, a television hanging in the corner became visible. Even though he hadn't paid the cartoons a lick of attention back at the house, it kept Tyler's attention now. *Go figure,* she thought. The audio was yet another indecipherable thread in the noisy fabric of the room, but the animations were engaging enough.

One show rolled into another. A second employee showed up to operate one of the vacant desks. And ninety minutes after first arriving, Charlene finally stepped up to the flaking vinyl counter.

The woman working had on a tan shirt that almost matched the beige on the walls. Aside from a slow blink, she made no move to address Charlene.

Still, Charlene's shoulders lowered in relief for the first time all morning. "Hi. I have a bit of a… situation. I need to talk to someone about what to do with an…" She lowered her voice so Tyler wouldn't hear. "An abandoned child."

The woman raised one brow. "Have you called the police?"

"No. No, I didn't think— I don't think this is that kind of situation."

"You should check to see if any missing children have been reported," she said flatly.

"He wouldn't have been reported missing. His mom is the one who abandoned him."

"And you know his mother?" the woman asked.

Charlene nodded. "I do."

"Do you know if the mother has any family you could contact who could take the boy in until the mother can be located?"

Guilt gnawed at her insides. "I suppose… well, I'm her family. I guess."

"You guess?"

"I'm her mother," Charlene explained. The loud room suddenly felt too quiet. They should really serve people in private offices. Talking about personal business in the open like this was uncomfortable.

The woman looked from Charlene to the visible top of Tyler's messy head. "You're the grandmother, then?"

Was that judgement in her voice or was Charlene imagining it?

"Technically," Charlene sighed. "I haven't seen my daughter in years. I didn't even know she had children. I just found out a few hours ago. If

I could just speak to someone, anyone. Maybe in an office. Somewhere more... private. That would really—"

The women suddenly reached into a drawer, pulled out a business card, and slid it across the counter to Charlene. "There's a number on this card you can call for counseling. If no one answers, leave a message. They'll get back to you within seventy-two hours. If there is an emergency, call the police."

Charlene blinked into the woman's unnaturally expressionless face. Was this part of their training? To behave like robots?

"I don't need counseling."

"You said you wanted to speak to someone about your situation. Our counselors can walk you through your options and offer guidance on what to do," she said. "They'll pair you with a caseworker as well, should you choose to use one."

"Can't you just do that?" Charlene asked. "I've been waiting in line for an hour and a half, and I just—"

"Call the number. Speak to a counselor," she repeated. "That's what I can do for you."

There was a tug on Charlene's pant leg. Tyler was shimmying side to side again, grabbing at the front of his own pants. "I need to potty."

"If that's all, I need to serve the next person in line," the woman said.

No, that wasn't all. Charlene wanted to argue. She wanted to stand in front of this clerk and demand more, better, different.

But she could tell by the woman's lifeless eyes that it wouldn't do any good.

Charlene didn't thank the clerk for her help as she left, mostly because she hadn't been helpful at all. She just turned around and started walking back towards the doors. Her mother would roll over in her grave at the rudeness, but Charlene didn't care.

The dark-haired man was still sitting in the chair by the door. As Charlene passed him, doing her best not to look him directly in the eyes, he shrugged.

"I hate to say 'I told you so…'"

The clear amusement in his voice said otherwise.

Charlene ignored him and walked through the doors and into the warm afternoon.

Fast food had been strictly forbidden when Margaret was growing up. "Fake, reconstituted garbage," Davy would say as they passed a burger joint, grease smoke pouring from the vents in the roof. "That isn't real food."

As Charlene bit into the foil-wrapped burger she'd just paid $3.79 for, she didn't care if it was real or not. She was starving. Fast food had been the fastest, cheapest way to solve that problem. Her stomach would pay for the indiscretion later, but it felt good to solve at least one problem. Even if it was the smallest problem currently on her plate.

The crunching coming from the backseat told her Tyler was content with her decision, too. What kid didn't love chicken nuggets and French fries, after all?

"I have to potty," Tyler said between chews.

Charlene groaned. How many times could a three-year-old pee in a day?

"Okay. Just another minute. We're basically home—" Charlene shook her head. "We're at my house. Just hold it for another minute."

She turned into the driveway and immediately hit the brakes. There was an unfamiliar car sitting there. A rental, by the looks of it.

Could it be the buyers back again? She didn't see anyone walking around the house, though. The windows of the SUV were too tinted to tell if anyone was inside.

She pulled the rest of the way into the drive, dumped her fast food trash on the floorboard of the passenger seat, and jumped out to free Tyler from the car seat.

"Please, please, please," she prayed under her breath. Her head was on a constant swivel as she crossed the yard.

In the hours since Chris and Katie had left the walkthrough, Charlene had thought of a thousand different better explanations she could have offered for why Tyler was crying in an upstairs bedroom. Maybe a better excuse could convince them to buy her house.

That's all she needed: one conversation. One conversation and she could sell the house where Davy had died and Margaret had deserted them. She could pay off the bills that hung over head.

One conversation, and Charlene could finally start over.

The SUV wasn't running and the front yard was clear. Charlene pulled her phone from her pocket to call Jamie and ask if the buyers had changed their minds. Then she heard someone nearby clear their throat.

Charlene looked up at her front porch and froze.

Tyler ran into the back of her leg and fell on his butt in the grass, but Charlene couldn't worry about that. She could barely breathe.

Because, for the second time in one day, one of the last people she ever expected to see was standing on her front porch, smiling at her.

It was a smile Charlene would know anywhere. Partly because it was a mirror image of her own.

Annette raised her hand in a meek wave. "Happy birthday, little sister. Long time, no see."

4

MID-AFTERNOON AT CHARLENE'S HOUSE

Charlene couldn't believe she was staring at her twin sister.

She squinted her eyes and tilted her head from side to side, expecting the vision in front of her to evaporate like a mirage.

What were the odds that her sister would show up for the first time in five years on the same day her daughter dropped a baby off on her porch?

No, no, no. It was too much.

But the mirage wouldn't go away.

Annette pulled a bouquet of white peonies out from behind her back. "I wish I could say these are from me, but a delivery driver just dropped them off. I signed for them as you. Hopefully, you don't mind."

Charlene opened her mouth to say... well, something. But before she could, Tyler gave his usual tug on her pant leg.

"I have to potty."

"Wait, who is that?" Annette asked.

"Tyler." It was the first thing Charlene had said to her sister. The first word she'd spoken to her in five years. She felt like she was floating outside her body.

This was all far, far too much.

"I have to potty," Tyler repeated with more urgency, squeezing his knees together.

"Okay. Come on, honey." Charlene patted his back and ushered him across the grass and up the steps. Annette moved out of the way to let them pass. When Charlene unlocked the front door, Annette followed them inside like it was perfectly normal.

"Who is Tyler?" she asked.

Tyler raised his little hand. "Me."

So his vocabulary did extend beyond needing to use the restroom. That was good to know.

Annette grabbed Charlene's shoulder and pulled her to a stop. "Is he *yours?*"

"No!" Charlene gritted her teeth and helped Tyler up the stairs. The carpet runner was still damp from the sink leak. She needed to roll it up and take it outside to dry before it hurt the finish.

"Then whose is he?"

Annette was *in* her house. The last time Annette had been there was... Christmas? Yes, Christmas. Three months before Davy's funeral. She and Frederick had skipped the wake.

"The flights are non-refundable," Annette had explained at the sanctuary.

"You can't stay?" Charlene had expected Annette to be there all day. To help her navigate all of the guests at the wake. To talk to Margaret, who'd always preferred her Aunt Annette.

"I want to, but we'd lose so much money. And Davy would understand. You know he would. He hated stuffy events like this."

Charlene had spent weeks preparing the funeral as Davy withered away in front of her. White wreaths crafted from roses and lilies and carnations hung from the end of the pews. Charlene had bent down to push one protruding rose back into place and pricked her finger on a thorn.

"Yeah, okay," she'd said. "I understand."

And she really had understood. Annette never much cared for Davy.

Despite the fact everyone else loved him, Annette and Frederick always kept their distance. As soon as Charlene and Davy had gotten married and had Margaret, Annette stopped visiting as often. Then she'd moved away. When she met Frederick and got married, her calls became even less frequent.

"Charlene! Whose kid is that?" Annette hissed from the hall. Then she picked up her feet and frowned. "And why is everything all wet?"

Tyler was sitting on the edge of the toilet so he wouldn't fall in, kicking his feet against the porcelain underside.

"There was a leak." Charlene swallowed. "And he is Margaret's son. She dropped him off this morning."

"Margaret has a kid?"

"So it seems."

Annette's eyes narrowed. "My birth announcement must have gotten lost in the mail. Excuse me for missing the big news."

"Both of ours must have gotten lost. Until this morning, I didn't know he existed, either."

And until two minutes ago, I never thought I'd see you again.

The world, it seemed, was full of mysteries.

"What does that mean?"

"She didn't tell me she had a kid," Charlene said.

"What do you mean she didn't tell you she had a kid?" Annette was practically shouting now. "She's your daughter!"

Charlene didn't want Tyler to hear. She moved to the other side of the door and lowered her voice. "She doesn't exactly talk to me. You should be familiar with the concept."

Annette's cheeks flushed red. "The phone works both ways."

This was no time to bring up the many unreturned phone calls Charlene had made in the months after Davy died. After enough went unanswered, Charlene got the point and stopped making them.

For Annette to show up here now and act like she had any right to know anything about Charlene's life was just cruel.

She pinched the bridge of her nose. A bottle of Tylenol was sitting in the bottom drawer of the bathroom vanity. After she took two of them, she'd have to move it to a higher shelf to make sure Tyler couldn't get into it. One of a million little things she had on her to-do list.

Charlene rolled her head on her shoulders and faced her sister. "What are you doing here, Annette? What's this about?"

Annette sucked in her cheeks and crossed her arms. "Frederick and I got in a fight. I needed to… cool off."

"You drove four and a half hours from Asheville to 'cool off'?"

"It was a big fight, okay? I just…" Annette looked like she was in physical pain trying to force the words out of her mouth. "I needed to get away and hide out somewhere Frederick wouldn't find me."

The realization was a slap in the face. "And you figured he would never look for you here. At your sister's house."

Annette didn't nod in agreement, but she didn't need to. The truth was plain enough. She might as well have thrown a dart at a map and traveled to wherever it stuck. Frederick would have the same amount of luck finding her either way.

"Look, can I stay? If not, I need to get going so I can find a hotel or something before it gets too late," she said. "I don't want to inconvenience your perfect life with my problems, so—"

Charlene bit back a sarcastic laugh and threw her arms out in a wild gesture. "Yes, welcome to my *perfect* life. Honestly, Annette…"

Tyler finished and Charlene helped him pull up his cotton shorts and wash his hands. He kept looking from Charlene to Annette, his little brow puzzled. "Are you the same?" he said finally.

"We're sisters," Annette explained gently. She bent down to his level and smiled. "We look the same, but I'm Annette."

"Net," Tyler repeated.

"Aunt Annette," she said slowly, annunciating each syllable.

"*Great* Aunt Annette," Charlene corrected.

She wrinkled her nose. "Don't say that. It makes me feel like I could star in *Golden Girls.*"

Despite everything that had happened that day, Charlene laughed.

Annette stood up, looking just as surprised as Charlene felt. Then she smiled softly.

Charlene helped Tyler down from the stepstool in front of the sink and followed him down the stairs. She didn't have any toys. There were breakables everywhere. And unless Tyler wanted to have leftover white bean and kale salad, Charlene didn't have anything edible for him in the house.

As soon as she made it to the base of the stairs, she spun around and faced her sister. "You can stay. *But—*"

"There are conditions?"

"But," Charlene continued, "you have to help me take care of Tyler. I don't know how long he's going to be here."

"You're the one who has actually raised a kid."

And look how well that turned out.

Charlene shrugged. "That's my condition. Take it or leave it."

Suddenly, Annette lunged past Charlene and snatched a gleaming letter opener out of Tyler's hands. She dropped it into the open drawer of the hallway buffet and closed it with her hip. Tyler tottered off to find something else to play with.

Annette looked at Charlene and sighed. "I'll take it, I guess. How hard can it be?"

A crash from the back of the house ended their conversation and sent them both running down the hallway.

After a disastrous few hours of play time and a dinner of boxed mac n' cheese and microwavable broccoli Charlene picked up on a run to Harris Teeter for supplies, Tyler was finally asleep in Charlene's bed.

"Where are you going to sleep?" Annette asked. She was slouched over the island, her dinner a congealed mass on the plate in front of her.

"In one of the guest rooms. You can take the other one. There's plenty of space."

"I forgot how big your house is."

Charlene wished she could forget. But walking past the empty rooms everyday was a stark reminder. She couldn't wait to sell the house. The bad memories had long since begun to outweigh the good.

"That's why I'm selling it. I don't need all this space." *And I need the money.*

"You could turn the spare rooms into a library. Or a craft room," Annette offered. "That's what I did."

"The last time I was in Asheville, they were all still bedrooms." Charlene had never understood why Annette and Frederick had bought a four-bedroom house. They'd lived in the place for ten years without ever touching the guest spaces. It seemed like such a waste.

Her sister shrugged. "I'm forty now. About time to pull the plug on the idea of having kids."

Charlene frowned. "But you two never wanted kids anyway. Right?"

"I wasn't completely against the idea. I... I could have been convinced." She bit her lower lip and then jumped up. "Wine time. I need a drink, do you?"

"Good heavens, yes." Charlene pointed to the pantry where Davy had hidden a wine refrigerator behind a false door years earlier. They'd had to put a lock on it when Margaret was in high school.

Annette poured them each a glass and sat back down. Something in the air had shifted. The five-year absence loomed between them.

"How have things been?" Charlene asked after an awkward pause. "Are you still at the bank?"

Annette shook her head. "I decided to finally put my degree to use. I'm teaching third grade at a small private school. I've been there a few years."

"Oh. I didn't know that."

"And you're still flipping houses, clearly." Annette gestured around at the remodeled kitchen. "How has that been?"

"Slow since Davy died," Charlene admitted. "He was able to do so much of the physical labor. It saved a lot of money. Now, I have to hire it all out and... well, you know how that goes."

Annette chuckled. "Not really. Our house is a new build." Suddenly, she frowned.

"What?"

"Oh, it's nothing. I just don't know if I can call it that anymore. *Our* house."

"So this fight with Frederick wasn't a small thing?"

"No," Annette murmured, swirling the red wine in her glass. "It wasn't a small thing."

She was being cagey and Charlene wanted to rattle the bars. She wanted her sister to talk to her. To really *talk* to her, the way they used to.

Last Charlene knew, Annette and Frederick were fine. Happy as could be. She didn't even have an inkling of what could have gone wrong between them.

"You don't have to tell me if you don't want," Charlene started. "It's your business, obviously. I'd just like to know how long you're expecting to stay so I can—"

"He has another house," Annette said suddenly.

Charlene blinked. "Another house?"

"And another woman. Another..." Annette's voice trailed off. She was blinking rapidly to keep her tears at bay.

"He was cheating on you?" After everything Margaret had put Charlene and Davy through, Charlene was all too aware that people were capable of anything. Still, Frederick hardly seemed like the type to have a secret life.

He worked in IT and had a biweekly game night with his coworkers. He listened to NPR podcasts instead of music.

It had always been a wonder that Frederick was able to snag the attention of Annette at all. So to accomplish that and then cheat on her? Unfathomable.

"For a few years, apparently." Annette pursed her lips. Her nostrils flared. "I was going through treatments. Taking shots and vitamins and pills, and… the entire time…"

"Treatments for what?" Even the hint of the "C" word sent Charlene's heart into her throat. She scanned Annette's body, looking for any sign of disease. Cancer had stolen so much from her already.

Annette looked up and blinked. "Oh, that's right. I guess you didn't know. I didn't tell many people. But I was doing fertility treatments."

"To have a kid?" She resisted the urge to slap her own forehead. *What else would fertility treatments be for, Charlene?* "Could you and Frederick not…?"

"God knew something I didn't," she finished with a shrug. "Everything works out the way it's supposed to, right? 'Live, learn, and leave it all behind,' as I like to say."

"I've never heard you say that before."

"It's a relatively new mantra." Annette flashed a smirk that didn't reach her eyes. "But I'm not the only one with drama. Looks like today has been a big day for you."

Classic deflection. Charlene had a million more questions, but it didn't seem like the right time to grill Annette. Not when she'd just come back. The last thing Charlene wanted was to push her away again.

"In more ways than one," Charlene muttered.

Annette leaned back in the barstool. "Well, spill it. What's with the little one?"

"I wish I knew. Margaret just left him on my doorstep with a note asking me to take care of him. That's all I know."

"Wow. That seems extreme. Even for Margaret." Annette glanced over at Charlene. "Sorry. I didn't mean—"

"It's fine. You're right."

"Do you know who the father is?"

"I don't have a clue," Charlene admitted. "When she left, she was still dating Steven, but—"

"Her drug dealer?"

Charlene snapped her attention to Annette. "How did you know that?"

"She stopped by my house a couple months after the funeral looking for money," Annette said. "She seemed pretty strung-out. She asked me not to tell you. I probably shouldn't have listened, but—"

"It wouldn't have made a difference either way. She still would have run off."

Charlene knew who her daughter was. For a long time, she hadn't wanted to admit it. Then Margaret robbed Charlene's wallet and ran. It only took five minutes of searching her emptied-out bedroom to find the discarded drug paraphernalia she left behind.

From that point on, there was no denying it: her daughter was an addict.

Annette sighed. "Honestly, she seemed desperate when I saw her. She broke down and told me the whole story. Explained who Steven was. Told me about the drugs. She seemed really regretful. I assumed she'd head home soon, which is why I didn't mention it."

"She didn't. I haven't seen her since Davy's funeral, either."

Either. The word cracked like a whip. Charlene could swear she saw Annette wince.

Charlene hurried to fill in the awkward silence. "Finding Tyler on the porch was at least confirmation she's alive. I didn't realize how worried I was about her until I had proof she was okay. Or, okay-ish, at least."

"And clear-headed enough to know she isn't capable of taking care of him," Annette suggested. "That's something. At least she brought Tyler here so you can take care of him."

Charlene's fingers tightened around the stem of her wine glass. "Well... I'm not so sure I'm that's true."

Annette's back straightened. "What do you mean?"

"I mean, I'm going to talk to a counselor at Social Services. See what my options are."

"Charlene..." Annette stared at her, blinking slowly. "He's your grandson."

If she'd been uncertain about whether the people in the DSS office were judging her, she wasn't uncertain about it now. There was no mistaking the tone in Annette's voice: she was appalled.

"A grandson I didn't even know I had until this morning."

"That doesn't change the facts."

"Like heck it doesn't!" Charlene took a deep breath, trying to settle the thundering in her chest. "I'm in the middle of a lot right now, okay? I have to figure out a new living situation and sell this house and... I can't handle raising another child."

"That's all some people want," Annette murmured.

"Which is why I'm checking into other options. I barely got through it the first time, and that was when Davy was alive. How am I supposed to—" Her voice caught in her throat. "I think someone else could be better for him. A happy family. Not... this."

Davy dead, his mom a runaway addict, and his grandma struggling to even take care of herself. Running through the list in her head, Charlene was more certain than ever.

Tyler needed to get out of here. He needed someone better.

She wasn't good enough for him.

"You should think about it. It's only been a day," Annette said. "You never know, he might grow on you and—"

"I'm tired." Charlene cut her sister off. She'd let Annette into her house for the first time in five years. That didn't mean she had to let her into her head. "It has been a long day."

There was a long pause before Annette answered. "Yeah, okay."

"You take Margaret's old room," Charlene said, dumping the rest of her wine into the sink. "I'm sure you remember where it is."

Without another word, Charlene turned on her heel and walked out of the room. For once, it felt good to be the one to do the leaving.

5

NEXT MORNING AT CHARLENE'S HOUSE

Sleep was hard to come by. The morning sun found her lying awake in bed. She stayed there until she heard Tyler's little feet padding across the hardwood floor in the room next door.

He'd slept through the night without waking. Based on Charlene's memories of Margaret, it seemed like a miracle. When she opened her door and saw him standing in the hallway, though, reality came crashing in.

"I pottied." His legs were spread wide, a damp spot in the middle.

Charlene hurried him into the bathroom, stripped off his pajamas, and put him in the tub.

"Do you wear diapers?" she asked as she bathed him.

Tyler splashed his hand in the water. "I wear big boy underwear."

"What about when you sleep?"

"I have Pull-Ups at night," he said.

Charlene added Pull-Ups to the running shopping list in her mind. For however long Tyler would be with her—up to seventy-two hours according to the woman at DSS, maybe longer—she would need supplies.

She washed him with her rose-scented body wash and then dressed him in the only other set of clean clothes Margaret had packed for him. Clothes were another item on her mental to-buy list.

"Do you want to go to the beach with me?" she asked. "We can go look at the water. Maybe see a turtle?"

His eyes widened. He looked so much like a little Margaret that Charlene had to catch her breath. "I want to look at turtles!"

Down in the kitchen, Charlene poured dry Cheerios into a plastic baggie. She filled one travel coffee mug with milk for Tyler and the other with coffee for herself. On her way out of the kitchen, she saw the note taped to the fridge.

Saw the bike in the garage and went for a ride. Be back later.

The note was in her sister's handwriting, but Charlene couldn't stop tears from gathering in the corners of her eyes. How many times had Davy written her notes like this?

The bike was his. He'd bought it on Craigslist a few years before his diagnosis.

"I'm well past the point of being able to rely on my metabolism," he'd said, patting his ever-so-slightly soft belly. "I think it would be good exercise for me."

"What, flipping houses isn't enough?" she'd asked.

Their job kept them on their feet and moving constantly. Hauling away junked cabinets, carting boxes of tile from the truck to the house and back, climbing up and down ladders all day to paint and hammer and clean. Neither of them usually required much additional exercise to stay trim.

"Walking on the beach is your outlet. This bike will be mine," he'd said, kissing her cheek before wheeling it into the garage.

It hadn't been touched in years.

"I'm hungry." Tyler's little voice, soft around the 'r' sounds, pulled her from her thoughts.

Charlene turned around just in time to see him slide his bag of cereal off the counter and shove his little fist inside.

"Is that good?" she asked, chuckling.

He nodded and shoved another handful in his mouth.

The walk down to the water took longer than normal. Tyler's legs were shorter, for one thing. For another, he stopped every few feet to point to a plant growing out of the ground or to try and shake out his sneakers.

"We'll have to get you some sandals so you won't get so much sand in your shoes," she said. Not to mention that his light-up shoes no longer lit up and were so small that his toes scrunched up at the top. "When we get down to the water, you can take them off and go barefoot."

The sun was already over the horizon, only the palest remnants of the pastel sunrise left behind. Elaine had probably already come and gone. They met up with each other most days, but not all the time. She probably assumed Charlene was sick or sleeping or busy with work. It would be a few days before she'd start to worry.

In the meantime, Charlene could think about how to explain Tyler. She'd been lying to Elaine about Margaret for years. Without really meaning to, she'd crafted an entire history for a fictional version of Margaret. A version that replaced all the nasty bits with pleasant lies. Charlene would have to undo all of that to explain how she'd instead come to leave her three-year-old son on his grandmother's porch.

As soon as they walked through a line of beach grass and into open sand, Charlene dropped down on her butt and sighed. "What a mess."

"Where?" Tyler spun in a circle.

Charlene chuckled and pointed to her head. "Up here."

Tyler looked at her for only a second before he dropped down into the sand next to her and yanked off his shoes and socks. When his toes squished in the sand for the first time, he smiled.

"Have you been to the beach before?" she asked.

Tyler shook his head. "I swimmed in a pool."

"At your house?"

He shrugged.

"Did you live in a house?"

"A house with a lot of houses."

"An apartment?" she guessed.

"A partment," he repeated slowly. "Miss Kelly has a partment, too."

"Is Miss Kelly a teacher?" He seemed young for school, even preschool, but it had been a long time since Charlene had thought about any of that. Things had probably changed since Margaret was his age.

"Miss Kelly lives next to us. She has pokey plants outside and I get in trouble if I touch them."

Charlene forgot what it was like to talk to little kids. The way their brains worked. How you can both be talking about the same thing without ever once understanding one another.

When Margaret was little, Charlene couldn't wait for her to get old enough for the two of them to talk. *Actually* talk. Charlene wanted to hear about her friends at school and the boys she liked and what music she enjoyed.

That never happened.

Turned out, they were destined to always misunderstand one another.

"Laney never gets in trouble. She goes to school. I can't go to school yet because I go to Miss Kelly's." He was jabbering away now, talking about a dog named Chester and the snacks Miss Kelly kept in the kitchen.

But Charlene was stuck on one point.

"Who is Laney?" She hadn't thought to wonder if Margaret had more kids. But it was possible. Horrifyingly possible. If she'd had a kid right after she'd left, that child could be in kindergarten. It was possible...

"Laney is my friend."

"Who is Laney's mommy?" Charlene asked. She had to focus hard to keep the desperation out of her voice.

Tyler picked up a broken seashell and held it to the sun. He squinted one eye. "Miss Kelly is Laney's mommy and Adam's mommy. Adam is a baby."

Charlene's shoulders sagged in relief. *Thank heavens.* At least she didn't have to worry about another kid being left on her doorstep. Not anytime soon, anyway.

Tyler dropped the shell and turned to Charlene. "I want to see turtles."

"Oh, right." Charlene pushed herself to standing and dusted sand from her pants. "It's right over here."

Wildlife service volunteers had marked the nest off with a few wooden stakes and caution tape, which Tyler immediately tried to limbo under.

"No, dear, don't step on them," she said, snatching him back. "They are just little babies. If you step on their nest, it could hurt them. And then they won't be able to crawl out and—"

For the first time, she noticed the all-too-familiar scuttle marks in the sand. The wavy trail of a baby sea turtle making its way to the ocean.

"Oh no."

Tyler turned around. "What?"

She pointed to the sand to show him. "A baby hatched already."

There was only one set of tracks, so it was probably just an early riser. There were more still in the nest. But Charlene was still disappointed to have missed it. She liked seeing the little critters off into the world.

"A baby?" Tyler set about searching the sand on hands and knees, looking for the turtle. He was occupied enough with the task that Charlene didn't bother telling him it was pointless. The turtle was long gone.

She plopped back down in the sand and watched the water while Tyler hunted for turtles. Once he got bored with that, he hunted for snakes and sharks and mermaids. He had quite the imagination.

"Fancy seeing you two here," came a sudden voice.

Charlene turned around to see Annette was coming down the beach path. She had on a pair of green leggings and a matching tank top. Her hair was pulled back into a tight ponytail.

"Aunt Net!" Tyler cooed.

"Glad to hear *Great* Aunt Annette didn't stick," Annette laughed. She sat down next to Charlene in the sand. "I saw you all walking down here as I was heading back to the house. But I also saw your coffee cup, so I had to swing by the house first. I'm in desperate need of caffeine."

"Didn't sleep well?"

Annette wrinkled her nose. "Not especially."

"Me neither," Charlene admitted.

"I suspect we both have a lot on our minds."

"I suspect you're right."

They fell into silence. The only thing to hear was Tyler chatting to himself and the water lapping against the shore.

After a few minutes, Tyler ran over holding a stick with a conch shell sitting on top. "A magic stick." He waved it around and then jabbed it towards Annette. "Freeze!"

Annette went stone-still, managing to hold her position even as Tyler fell into a fit of giggles. Eventually, he unfroze her and wandered off to make more "magic sticks."

"He's a cute kid," Annette sighed. "Makes me think a lot of Margaret."

"It's the eyes. They're exactly the same."

Annette hummed her agreement. "It must make it hard to let him go."

Charlene couldn't tell if that was a jab or an observation. Either way, Annette was right. If she was being honest, Charlene was trying not to look too closely at Tyler. It made her heart hurt.

"I don't have a choice."

"Of course you do. You can keep him or give him away. There's your choice."

"Like it's that easy," Charlene snapped. "There's a lot more to consider."

"Margaret left him with you for a reason."

"Yeah, because there was no one else! Believe me, Margaret is the last person who would accuse me of being a great parent."

Annette turned. "Come on, Char. You know that's not true."

"No, it's fine. I accepted it a long time ago. When she left."

"There were other things going on. The drugs and Davy's death and—"

"And I'm her mom," Charlene interrupted. "I should have noticed. But I didn't. I failed her. I just... I don't want to fail him."

When Margaret hit high school, it was like she became a new person. Maybe there were signs before then that Charlene had missed; maybe not. But whichever it was, she woke up one day and it was like there was a different person in her daughter's body. Missing curfew, sneaking out, coming home reeking of vodka.

Davy had been the one to talk to her. "She promised she'd get her act together," he said afterwards. He'd been in her bedroom for almost an hour. Charlene hadn't been invited to the conversation.

"What does that even mean?" Charlene asked.

"Exactly what I said. She is going to pull it together. No more drinking, no more partying. She was crying."

Charlene had raised a brow. "Crying doesn't mean she's sorry she did it. She might just be sorry she got caught."

"She meant it, Char," he'd insisted. "Believe me—she'll be fine."

And outwardly, Margaret had been.

Until Davy died and she ran off. Then Charlene found out the truth: Margaret had kept right on doing exactly what she wanted. She just found better ways to hide it.

"Well," Annette said softly, "what are you going to do then?"

Charlene was sick of weighing her options. She went from one to the next to the next and right back to the first one again, over and over like a teacup ride at the fair. It made her nauseous. "I have no way of getting in touch with Margaret. I can't keep him."

"Disagree," Annette said quickly. "But continue."

"... So I'm going to call DSS and talk to a counselor. See what the other options are."

"Sounds like adoption is all that's left."

Charlene took a deep breath. "Sounds like it."

Tyler was creeping closer to the water in his search for more shells, but he was still far enough away that Charlene wasn't worried yet. She could see his little footprints dotting the sand like the baby turtle's had. A little trail showing where he'd been.

Charlene wondered where his path would lead him.

And how far from her it would take him away.

Charlene had been on hold with DSS almost as long as she'd waited in line the day before. But at least this time she was free to pace around without worrying about her spot in line.

Tyler was upstairs napping. Annette had run out to The Village Bookseller in Mt. Pleasant.

"I can't sleep unless I read a book before bed, and Davy's library of spy novels isn't going to cut it," she'd said. "I need romance. Unrealistically swoony heroes. Happily-ever-afters."

"Don't we all!" Charlene had called after her.

Charlene assumed she'd call DSS and then still have time to work on the bathroom sink upstairs or clean up the crumbs from lunch that were scattered under the dining room table. Instead, the minutes ticked past relentlessly while awful hold music played. Tyler would be up soon and she still hadn't spoken to a single human being. Just a robotic answering machine.

Finally, just as she was about to set the phone down so she could run up to the bathroom, the hold music cut and a woman's voice picked up. "Hello?"

"Hello!" Charlene rasped. She cleared her throat and tried again. "Hi. Hello."

"This is Darlene with the Department of Social Services. How may I help you?"

"I was in yesterday to try and speak to someone and a receptionist gave me this number to call. Something about a counselor. I don't need a counselor, per se," she explained. "I am just in a situation and I need someone to explain what my options are."

"Meeting with a counselor is the standard procedure," the woman said. "Every situation is different, so we like to meet with people on a one-on-one basis to ensure we have a full understanding. Are you or anyone else in danger?"

"No, no. Nothing like that."

"Okay." The woman clicked her tongue. "Well, then the soonest I'm going to be able to fit you in is in two weeks."

Charlene's mouth fell open. "Two weeks? From today?"

"From tomorrow, actually," the woman said. "Sorry, but we've been short-staffed and busy. Will that work for you?"

Charlene wanted to say 'no.' But technically, she didn't have a time frame. Charlene couldn't ruin Tyler in only two weeks. And aside from her own desire to sort this mess out as soon as possible and get back to selling her house, there was no reason she couldn't keep Tyler. Money was tight, but what were a few more credit card charges in the meantime?

Especially since the next option for him would likely be a foster home. He'd had enough change as it was. There was no need to put him through more. Annette would probably disown her again if she tried something like that anyway.

Charlene sighed. "Okay, but is there some kind of waitlist? Like, a way to be bumped up if there is a cancellation or an opening?"

"Your appointment will put you on the waiting list," the woman confirmed. "If there is an opening, we'll contact you in appointment order."

The woman hadn't provided any better news than the woman at the DSS office the day before, but at least she'd been slightly more pleasant about it. Which earned her a "thank you very much" from Charlene.

As soon as she hung up, Charlene dropped down into a kitchen barstool.

For the time being, Tyler was here to stay.

6

LATE AFTERNOON AT CHARLENE'S HOUSE

"You didn't need to buy him anything, Annette. It's too much."

Charlene eyed the stack of picture books sitting next to Tyler, nearly as tall as he was.

"Tyler doesn't think it's too much." Annette sipped her sweet tea. "Besides, it has been years since I've bought a gift for a kid. All of my friends' children are practically grown now. Margaret, too, obviously. This is my only chance."

When Annette left the bookstore in Mount Pleasant, she'd stopped in at a children's boutique nearby. She bought Tyler four outfits, swim trunks, sandals, and a new pair of green dinosaur light-up sneakers. Charlene had caught a glimpse of the price tags before Annette could tear them off. Money clearly wasn't an object for her twin sister.

"I just want you to know he isn't your responsibility. I'm the one who should be dealing with this. I know I said you had to help me if you wanted to stay, but I meant with watching him. You don't need to buy him anything."

Annette turned to Charlene with a raised brow. "You talk about him like he's one of those robotic babies they hand out for Home Ec assignments in high school."

"We had bags of flour," Charlene corrected. "And you spilled yours all over the living room carpet."

Annette waved the memory away. "You know what I mean. He's a real, living, breathing human, Charlene. And it takes a village."

"To *raise* a child," Charlene corrected. "It takes a village to *raise* a child. I'm just… caretaking."

Annette opened her mouth to argue, but before she could, a voice interrupted. "There you are!"

Charlene looked up just as Elaine cut across her grass. She had on a wide-brimmed sun hat, which she pulled off immediately to get a better look at the front porch. Her eyes bounced from Charlene to Annette to Tyler like a pinball machine.

The time Charlene had thought she had to come up with an explanation suddenly evaporated. Immediately, her stomach twisted with nerves.

"This explains why I missed you this morning," Elaine said. "You have visitors! Annette, how lovely to see you."

Annette stood up and picked her way around Tyler. She pulled Elaine into a hug. "It's been too long. How have you been?"

"Oh, you know me. Staying busy doing nothing. What about you?"

Annette filled her in on her new job at the private school, conspicuously leaving out any mention of Frederick. Elaine either didn't notice or didn't care.

"… I tried Pilates a couple years ago and it nearly hobbled me." Elaine clutched dramatically at her back. "If you think you're hurting now, wait until you're a member of the Over-Fifty Club."

"Yoga," Annette insisted. "Pilates is a young person's game. Yoga is much better for my stiff muscles."

"I've found sitting on the couch to be the best for my sore joints," Charlene teased.

She was grateful no one had mentioned Tyler yet. Maybe Charlene wouldn't have to explain anything at all.

Elaine snorted. "Please. You are always on the go. Every time I see you, you're hammering this or painting that or rushing out to the hardware store for this, that, and the other. I almost didn't recognize you sitting down."

"She's not wrong," Annette agreed. "And now with Tyler around, you have even less time for sitting."

Charlene did her best to hide her wince.

"I was about to ask who this handsome young man was," Elaine said. He'd finally looked up long enough to see there was nothing especially interesting going on and then turned his attention back to his books.

"That's Tyler." Charlene put a hint of finality in her voice. As though she'd just answered any question anyone could ever have about Tyler.

"He's adorable," Elaine cooed. "Who does he belong to?"

"Oh, well..." Charlene sat forward in her chair. She needed to brace herself for this. At some point, the truth would come out. But why did it have to be today? "He's actually—"

"My nephew," Annette cut in coolly. "We're here visiting for a few days. He's a handful, so I had to call in Charlene for reinforcements."

Another lie, sort of. But one Charlene was grateful for.

"He doesn't look like a handful. He looks like a sweetheart."

"He's both," Annette laughed.

Elaine smiled. "The best kids are. I don't know how long you're here for, but if you need anyone to watch him, I'd be happy to."

"Oh no, we couldn't ask that of you," Charlene said.

"We absolutely could ask it of her," Annette teased.

"It would be my pleasure! I love kids."

"That's perfect," Annette said. "Because I've been in town for two days and we haven't been down to The Windjammer yet."

Elaine gasped like a deadly sin had been committed. "Then that settles it. You two need to go out for a drink, and I need to spend some quality time with this little sweetie."

"Elaine, really. You don't need to."

"Shush." Annette narrowed her eyes at Charlene. "You heard her. It's settled. We're going out."

Charlene didn't feel much like going out. Partly because she hadn't been "out" in years. And partly because, with her recent string of bad luck, the balcony at The Windjammer was likely to collapse the moment she stepped onto it.

But she recognized the determined set to Annette's mouth. The narrowing in her eyes. There would be no arguing with her now.

Charlene sighed. "Fine. One drink. Nothing more."

EVENING AT THE WINDJAMMER

Charlene felt cute leaving the house in her white capris and a denim sleeveless shirt. Now that they were at The Windjammer, though, she felt ancient.

"I look like a grandma," she complained.

"Well, you are a grandma."

Oh. Right.

"You know what I mean," she said.

They were standing at the bar inside waiting on their drinks. Annette had her heart set on drinking on the balcony, so Charlene was trying her best to think happy thoughts. Thoughts that didn't involve collapsing balconies or troubled daughters or abandoned children. At least for a couple hours.

"We look hot." Annette bumped Charlene's hip with her own.

"Easy for you to say." Annette must have anticipated at least a few nights out while she was on the island, because she'd packed all the right clothes. She had on a salmon-colored stretchy dress with a thin white cardigan wrapped around her waist. She looked effortlessly chic.

The bartender was a middle-aged man with a goatee and a vintage rock t-shirt on. He raised a flirtatious brow at Annette as he slid two glasses of wine to her. Annette handed one to Charlene, barely noticing.

"Remember how much of a hit we used to be at parties? The Wilson Wonders, they used to call us!"

"That's what *you* used to call us," Charlene laughed. "And I hated that nickname. It was embarrassing."

"But accurate. Guys used to flock to us."

"We did alright for ourselves," Charlene admitted with a sly smile.

Annette hummed in agreement. "That we did. Before you met Davy and became staunchly monogamous."

"Excuse me for falling in love." Charlene smiled. But she wondered if there was truth in the jab. If Annette resented Charlene for falling in love so young. For starting a family before she was ready.

Up until that point, they'd done everything together. Even their first kisses happened on the same night. Then, suddenly, Charlene met Davy, got married, and had Margaret in the span of two years. It was a whirlwind. But Annette hadn't been on the same timeline as Charlene. Maybe that was why she'd distanced herself from Charlene and Davy and all their marital bliss.

"Falling in love," Annette sighed. "It happens to the best of us."

They claimed a table near the wooden railing outside. Condensation was already sliding down the sides of their glasses thanks to the balmy evening. But the fresh sea air felt nice no matter the temperature.

The beach stage was empty tonight, but scattered crowds of people still stood in the sand in front of it, drinking and laughing. Country music was pumping through the speakers from inside. A few brave souls were even dancing.

One particularly boisterous group of men were making their way around to the various groups, trying to lure women into dancing. When they struck out with everyone on the ground, they turned their attention to the balcony. A man in a backwards baseball cap and a tank top pointed up at Charlene and Annette's table.

"Come on down and dance, ladies," he called. "We don't bite."

Charlene wrinkled her nose, but Annette tossed her head back and cackled. Then she leaned over the railing. "You might not, but we do."

"Don't threaten me with a good time! Why don't you come show us?"

"Maybe after two more rounds of these," Annette said, holding up her glass. "If you're lucky."

"I am *not* going down there," Charlene protested as the man sauntered off. "No matter how many rounds he sends up."

"Me neither," Annette agreed. "Tonight is not his lucky night."

When a waitress carried up two more glasses of wine, courtesy of Annette's new friend, Annette lifted her glass in a toast to the man in the sand. Then she toasted Charlene.

"The Wilson Wonders strike again."

Charlene groaned, but couldn't hold back a laugh.

As they sipped on their drinks, Annette smiled down at the man in the baseball hat a few more times. Eventually, he succeeded in snaring another woman in a dance and forgot all about them. That was fine with Charlene. She hadn't danced with a man since Davy died. This was not the week to start.

"Is there any chance you'll forgive Frederick?"

"Whoa." Annette turned, eyes wide. "Coming at me out of nowhere with a heavy hitter."

"Feels like heavy hitters are all we've had lately."

"I guess so, but what brought that on?"

Charlene tipped her head towards where the man was now twirling a young woman in a white bikini cover-up around the floor. "For a married woman, you seemed pretty flirtatious with that guy. It got me thinking."

"Frederick didn't let marriage stop him." There was acid in her voice. But as quickly as it appeared, it faded away. "Honestly, I don't know. I haven't decided. That's why I'm here. To clear my head. Think."

"And take care of a three-year-old," Charlene added. "I'm sure that was on your itinerary."

"It's been a fun surprise. Maybe a blessing, even." Annette smiled. "Kids have a way of making it hard to focus on your own problems, don't you think?"

Focusing on her own problems is all Charlene had done recently. But she didn't want to admit as much to Annette. Before she could say anything else, someone approached their table.

Unfortunately, it was a face she recognized.

"Small world," the rude man from the DSS office said. He pressed a hand flat to his chest. "Noah, in case you've forgotten."

"You aren't the kind of person one forgets," Annette interjected. If they'd been in a cartoon, Annette would have wolf-whistled and then let her tongue flop out of her mouth onto the floor.

Noah looked over and Charlene saw the shock register on his face. He glanced from Annette to Charlene and back again. Finally, he shook his head and laughed. "Either I've had too much to drink or there are two of you."

"We're sisters," Annette grinned. "Some call us the Wilson Wonders, but—"

"No, they don't. No one calls us that."

Noah smiled. "I just want to know which of you is called Charlene."

Charlene raised her hand.

"I was right on the first try. Good for me."

Annette offered her hand to shake. "I'm her sister, Annette. How do you two know one another?"

"Oh, we go way back," he said. "We spent a few hours together just the other day."

Annette's eyes went wide. "Excuse me?"

"He was at the Department of Social Services when I was there," Charlene mumbled.

"I warned her not to waste her time waiting in line and call instead. She didn't listen."

"She rarely does," Annette drawled.

He was being charming right now. To Annette, at least. And he was frustratingly handsome. More handsome than someone with his prickly temperament had any right to be.

Charlene was suddenly struck with the thought of how awful it would be for Annette to be interested in this rude man. For them to date. To get married.

"The website said walk-ins were welcome," Charlene explained. "And why have a lobby that's open to the public if the only way to get anything done is to call?"

"Did you call then?" Noah asked. "Were you able to get everything sorted out?"

Charlene narrowed her eyes. "I took care of my business, thanks." She didn't know why he cared so much.

Annette turned. "You did? About Tyler, you mean?"

"I have an appointment in two weeks, but I asked to be contacted if anything else opened up in the meantime," Charlene said quietly. Noah didn't need to know anything else about her business.

"There are cancellations all the time," he said. "I'm sure you'll get a call in the next couple days."

"Really?" Charlene couldn't keep the hope out of her voice.

Noah smiled. "Definitely."

"That's amazing."

"Glad to be the bearer of good news," he said. "If you're interested, I can also be the bearer of drinks. Next round on me?"

Alarm bells went off in Charlene's head. Noah had shifted from surly to flirty in an instant. And Charlene had no interest in leading the man on.

"Actually, I think it's about time we get going." Charlene glanced at her watch without really seeing the time. "Don't you think, Annette?"

Annette finished the wine in the bottom of her glass in one gulp and then stood up. "Yeah. I'm ready to go."

Noah seemed surprised. *Probably not used to rejection,* Charlene thought. But he stepped aside to let the women pass and then offered a final wave before they went inside.

"Good luck with everything," he called.

Charlene gave him a tense wave and then left him marooned on the balcony.

"He was a dream," Elaine said about Tyler when they got back to the house. "I could barely keep up with how quickly his little mind moved, but it was so fun. And he went right to sleep without a fight. What a sweet boy."

"The sweetest," Annette agreed. "Thanks again for watching him."

"Of course. I hope you two had a good time. Call me anytime you need anything. I'd love to watch him again."

Charlene turned on the porch light and watched Elaine safely to her car. As soon as she was gone, she flicked off the light and locked the front door.

When she turned around and found Annette standing only a few feet away from her, she yelped in surprise. "You scared me!" Charlene tried to walk around her sister, but Annette cut her off. "What's going on?"

"Tyler isn't a flip house, Charlene," she said somberly.

Charlene frowned. "What does that mean?"

"He isn't something for you to take in, fix up, and then sell to the highest bidder. He's a little boy."

"Where is this coming from?"

"'*I took care of my business,*'" Annette mocked in a high-pitched voice that was apparently supposed to mimic Charlene's. "He isn't a project. He's a person. *Your grandson.*"

"I didn't mean it like that. I just didn't want Noah to know anything about my business."

"There you go again," Annette snapped. "*Your* business. But this isn't your business. This is Tyler's life. His entire future. And you're throwing it away."

Charlene took a step back as though she'd been slapped. She might as well have been. The words stung just the same.

"I'm not throwing him away. Margaret did that. I'm doing what's best for him."

"And you really think being raised by strangers would be better for him than knowing where he came from? Than being with family?"

Charlene crossed her arms. "I've already told you how I feel. I can't do it."

"Well, neither can I." Annette turned on her heel and marched towards the steps.

As much as Charlene wanted the conversation to be over, she followed her sister. "What does that mean?"

Annette spun around, looking down at Charlene from a few steps up. "It means I can't sit here and watch you dump this little boy off like he's a bag of old clothes you want to donate. Not when you and I both know you can take care of him. You just don't want to."

"So you're leaving?"

"I'm leaving," Annette said. "I'll go get a motel in Mount Pleasant for tonight and then—"

"You're not going anywhere tonight," Charlene said firmly. "We've been drinking. You aren't thinking clearly."

Annette's eyes narrowed. "Don't speak for me. I'm thinking clearly enough. You're the one who is all," she pointed to her head and spazzed her hands in the air like static electricity, "messed up."

Charlene knew how to get along with her sister. She also knew how to not see her for years at a time. She wasn't sure how to do *this*.

"If you want to get away from me, going up to your room and sleeping is the fastest option. If you wake up tomorrow and still want to leave, I'll help you pack. Okay?"

Annette stared down at her for a few seconds. Her chest heaved and her nostrils flared. Finally, she nodded once and stomped up the stairs.

Charlene sighed. She'd bought herself one more night. One more night of having her sister in her life.

The question was: how long could it last?

7

NEXT MORNING AT CHARLENE'S HOUSE

It was a restless night. When Charlene's alarm went off at six-thirty, she nearly threw her phone through the window. When it started ringing again what felt like only ten minutes later, she slapped at her nightstand and blindly clicked buttons. But the ringing wouldn't stop.

Finally, she picked up her phone and realized it wouldn't stop because it wasn't an alarm; it was a phone call. Also, it was past eight AM.

The number was unknown, but Charlene had been answering everything the last few days. She'd spoken to more telemarketers in forty-eight hours than she had in her entire life. Hoping each time it would be Margaret instead.

It never was.

"Hello?" she rasped into the phone. Her throat was dry. When she sat up, the room swam.

How long had it been since she'd been hungover? She could go her entire life without ever feeling this way again and it would still be too soon.

"Is anyone there?" she said again when no one answered.

"Oh, hi. Sorry," a woman said. "I guess I didn't hear you. Is this Charlene Wilson?"

Charlene's back straightened. "It is. And who is this?"

"I'm with the Department of Social Services. I have written here that you have an appointment scheduled in two weeks with a counselor. But there was a cancellation and we have an opening—"

"I'll take it!"

"—in half an hour," the woman finished.

"Oh." Charlene didn't need a mirror to know she was a mess. Her eyes felt crusty and puffy. Her skin was slicked with the alcohol her body had been trying to sweat out overnight. She smelled sour.

"If the address you provided is correct, we have a caseworker who could meet you at your house. They live in the area."

"In half an hour?" Charlene confirmed.

"Yes. I know it's last minute. That's why everyone has passed on the time slot so far. If you'd like to keep your original appointment, that is fine. I can just—"

"No, I'll still take it." Charlene jumped out of bed and hurried across the hall into the bathroom. "Put my name down. I'll be ready."

She hung up with the woman and stepped immediately into the shower. The water hadn't had time to warm up yet, so it was breathtakingly cold. Charlene winced and dunked her head under it. That should wake her up.

There was no time for lather, rinse, repeat. Or shaving. Or a full body wash. Charlene hustled through the basics as fast as she could and hurried out.

She was still soaked when she stepped out of the shower, and her foot slipped across the slick tile floor. Charlene cried out and gripped the sink for balance.

A few seconds later, Annette's voice sounded through the door. "Are you okay?"

Charlene wrapped her towel around her, opened the door, and hurried past Annette and back into her room. "I'm fine, but I need you to watch Tyler for me this morning. A caseworker is going to be here in—" She looked at the time on her phone and whimpered, "fifteen minutes."

"Looks like you're prepared."

There wasn't time to explain the situation. "Can you do it or…?"

"Yes, obviously," Annette snapped. "Some of us are happy to spend time with Tyler."

That comment deserved a retort. But when Charlene turned around to offer one, Annette was already gone.

She managed to tug on a pair of jeans and a plain blue t-shirt, comb through her wet hair, and apply deodorant before there was a knock on the front door.

Great. Just how I wanted to meet the caseworker, she thought. But at least she would smell like something other than stale alcohol. That counted for something.

Charlene slipped into a pair of sandals and hustled down the stairs. She paused in front of the door to catch her breath and tuck a strand of damp hair behind her ear. Then she opened it.

"Hello! Sorry I'm such a mess, but—"

"So it is you," a familiar deep voice said.

Charlene's eyes scanned slowly from the clipboard in the man's hand to his neatly buttoned shirt, all the way up to his salt and pepper hair.

Why was she being punished this way?

"Noah?" she groaned.

"Yes, I'm happy to see you, too," he said. "I don't meet many people named Charlene. When I got the assignment this morning, I thought I might be seeing you again."

"You work at the Department of Social Services?" It made sense. Why else would he have been lurking around the building? But somehow, Charlene hadn't even considered it a possibility.

Now, here he was.

"That I do," he said. "I'm the caseworker assigned to Tyler's case. And I actually have a full schedule today. Do you mind if I come in or should I give you another minute to, uh, ready yourself?"

If Charlene thought there was a real possibility that she could cancel this meeting, keep her original appointment in two weeks, and be assigned a different caseworker, then she would have slammed the door right in Noah's face.

But her luck wasn't nearly that good. So instead, she stood to the side and ushered Noah into her home.

"We can sit at the table. I'll make coffee."

Lord knew she needed it today.

"Perfect. I take mine black, thanks."

Charlene rolled her eyes. He didn't need to be tolerable; he just needed to be good at his job.

For her sake—and Tyler's—she hoped he was.

Noah drank his coffee slowly. Charlene inhaled hers.

Being hungover any day would be bad enough, but today? In front of Noah? It was more like a nightmare. The last thing Charlene wanted was to give him yet another reason to look down on her. She wanted her head on straight so she could explain her situation clearly and effectively.

"What did you do after you left The Windjammer last night?"

"I came home," she said.

"Is that so? No nightcaps?"

"I did!" she insisted. "What, is that something you'll have to make note of on your fancy clipboard? *'Respondent had two glasses of wine on a weeknight'*?"

He smiled. "Nothing of the sort."

"Good. Because you were there, too," she reminded him. He looked remarkably more put together than she did, though.

"And more grateful every second that I was." He took a slow sip of his coffee and looked at her over the rim. "It was nice seeing you."

She did not have the mental acuity to translate that line. "I thought you had a full schedule today?"

"That I do." He sat up a little straighter and scanned the papers in front of him. "The only note I have in my file is that Tyler was abandoned by his mother on your doorstep. Is that right?"

Charlene interlaced her fingers on the tabletop. "That's right. Two mornings ago."

His pen scratched across the clipboard. "And you're related to the mother?"

"I'm the mother."

Noah's eyebrows shot up. "I'm sorry, do you mean—"

"Oh, no." Charlene realized all at once what she'd said. "No, I'm not *the* mother. I'm not Tyler's mother. I'm her mother. The mother's mother." She sighed and ran a hand through her damp hair to push it back from her face. "Tyler's mom is my daughter."

Noah's shoulders relaxed slightly. "You're Tyler's grandmother."

Technically. "Yes. I am."

"And is there a grandfather in the picture?"

God, how Charlene wished there was! Davy would know what to do.

"No. It's just me."

Another scratch across his clipboard, this one longer than the last. Then he sat the clipboard down and leaned back in the chair. His fingertips drummed against the handle of his coffee mug. "What do you know about your daughter and her current situation?"

Charlene knew he was just doing his job. But she couldn't help imagining the heat of an overhead light shining down on her. Was Noah the good cop or the bad cop?

"Currently, I don't know anything. I haven't spoken to her in… a long time."

"How long?"

"A few years."

"How many years?"

Charlene sighed. "It was five years in… in March, I guess."

"Almost five and a half years, then." Noah leaned forward to pick up his pen and make another note.

Charlene didn't see the need to be that specific. Five years was long enough, wasn't it? A long time for any mother to go without speaking to her child. What were a few extra months on top?

"Do you have any idea why she may have abandoned her son?" Noah asked.

The amused smile he'd worn at the DSS office was gone now. Charlene couldn't decide if she missed it or not. At least when she'd thought he was laughing at her, she had a reason to dislike him. She'd prefer that over being pitied.

"I mean, who knows?" Charlene wrapped her hands around her coffee mug before she realized it was empty. Immediately, she spun away from the table for a refill. "Margaret was always impulsive."

Understatement of the year. How many once-used soccer cleats did Charlene still have in her storage unit? How many piano keyboards with one session's fingerprints on them? Margaret picked up and dropped hobbies like she was juggling.

Until the drugs. That one stuck.

"And there were... drugs," she added reluctantly. "I didn't find out about that until after she ran away."

"She ran away?" Another scribble on his clipboard. "When was that?"

"Five years ago." Charlene shook her head. "I mean, five and a half years ago. She was eighteen. I couldn't exactly stop her. I searched her room once she was gone and found a small stash. Some supplies. I don't know if she's still using, but... well, I wouldn't be surprised."

Charlene's face was burning hot. *This interview is for Margaret and Tyler, not you. You're not on trial.*

Noah made a soft humming noise in the back of his throat and shook his head as he wrote things down. His coffee sat abandoned on the table. When he sat back in his chair, his gray-blue eyes were once again on Charlene.

"And you haven't had any contact with her since then?"

"Not aside from the note she left Tyler with," Charlene said. "And even that was brief, to say the least."

"No one has contacted you in regards to any legal decisions Margaret may have made regarding Tyler?"

Charlene frowned. "Should they have?"

Noah stared at her for a moment too long. He bit his lip before he started talking. "It seems you might not be aware that Margaret went before a judge this week."

Charlene blinked. "She what?"

"She sought to terminate her rights as Tyler's parent," he explained. "She submitted proof that she left the child in your care. She doesn't want him."

At that moment, Charlene heard little footsteps upstairs. Tyler was awake.

And his mother didn't want him.

That should have been obvious to Charlene when she'd opened her door and found the little boy standing on her front porch. But it hadn't sunk in fully. Not until now.

"Going the legal route could absolve her from any fines or legal charges," Noah continued. "It could all just be an attempt to protect herself. But regardless, it seems as though the judge will likely agree to terminate her rights. That would give you the opportunity to become his legal guardian."

After pouring her coffee, Charlene had been standing against the counter. But suddenly, her legs felt weak. She stumbled forward to the table and dropped into a chair. "I'm his legal—?"

"You could be if you choose. We prefer to place children with family when possible, so I would encourage you to consider it. Ultimately, it's your choice, of course."

"What would you do?" The words were out of Charlene's mouth before she could stop them. She shook her head. "I'm sorry. That wasn't… That's inappropriate. I'm just—I think I'm in shock. Maybe."

She laughed, but it came out sounding unhinged. She took a sip of coffee to shut herself up.

"It's okay," Noah said warmly. "This is a lot to take in. Believe me, I get it."

The way he said it hinted at... something. What exactly that something was, Charlene couldn't say.

"You have a lot of personal experience with this kind of thing?" she asked.

"Something like that."

He didn't elaborate. "Oh," Charlene said. "Right."

"I don't usually offer my personal opinion," he added. "My job is to be a neutral party."

Charlene waved her hands. "I get it. Entirely. Don't mention it again. I'm sorry I asked."

"But..." He leaned forward, voice low. "I can tell you that, in my experience, people regret the things they don't do a whole lot more than the things they do."

"Okay." Charlene nodded, trying to absorb the advice. If it could even be called that.

"Did that help?"

She started to nod and then slouched forward in defeat. "Honestly, no. Not even a little bit."

Noah laughed. "Yeah, it can really work both ways. Which is why I can offer it up as advice."

"Because it's useless?"

"Because it only means whatever you make of it." He smiled and then reached into his pocket. He pulled out a small card and slid it across the table. "And off the record, I'd tell you to look into this."

Charlene picked up the card and squinted at it to read the fine print. Turning forty-five meant she needed reading glasses, apparently.

"Safe Haven Adoption Agency," she read aloud.

"It's a private adoption agency. They work much faster than the state."

Charlene turned the card between her fingers. "If I didn't know any better, I'd think you were trying to get rid of me."

He shuffled a few papers together and clipped them onto his board. "My job is to make sure the decisions being made are in the best interest of the child. And from what I can see here, that's what you're trying to do for Tyler."

"You think so?" Charlene sounded desperate. Like she was fishing for a compliment. But after her argument with Annette last night, her confidence was shaken. She could use the boost.

He nodded. "Taking care of a child is a massive responsibility. It seems like you're aware of that. You're treating the situation with care and consideration."

"I'm trying."

Noah reached out and patted her shoulder. It was a brief touch, but Charlene felt a zing of energy pass between them. "Just think about what's in Tyler's best interest. So long as that is your focus, I'm sure you'll make the right choice."

The right choice. As if there were only one. As if there were one at all.

"More coffee?" she offered. Half an hour ago, she wanted to slam the door in his face. Now she was offering him coffee. What was wrong with her?

"I wish." Noah checked his watch. "But I really do have a full schedule."

"Oh, right. I kind of forgot this is your job."

"This would be a rather weird first date, wouldn't it?" he asked.

Charlene shrugged. "There have been weirder."

Noah's mouth tilted into a smirk. "On a day I have more time, I'd love to expand on that. Unfortunately, I have another meeting in fifteen minutes."

"I feel so used," Charlene teased in a classic Hollywood accent as she led him to the front door.

"If it helps, I'm positive this will be my favorite appointment of the day."

"You say that to everyone, I'm sure."

He stepped onto the porch and looked back over his shoulder. His brown eyes glimmered gold in the morning light. "I promise you, I don't."

When Charlene finally did shut the door on Noah, she found it much less satisfying than she'd assumed it would be. A teeny tiny part of her even wished he could have stayed.

8

MORNING AT CHARLENE'S HOUSE

As soon as Noah left, Charlene turned and found Annette on the stairs, in more or less the same place she'd been standing last night during their fight.

"What did he say?"

Charlene sighed. "Margaret went to a judge to sign away her parental rights. She wanted me to be named his guardian."

"Oh."

"Yeah. Lots to process." Charlene slid the dead bolt into place and drummed her fingers on the cool metal. "But it's my choice, obviously."

"And what are you gonna do?"

Charlene leaned back against the door. It wasn't even nine in the morning and she needed a nap. "The judge hasn't even terminated her rights yet."

"But does Noah think they will?"

Charlene nodded. "Likely."

"So?"

"You already know what I want to do, Annette."

"Then I don't know why you won't just tell me," she snapped. "Unless you're ashamed to say it out loud."

"I'm not ash—You can't shame me into a decision. You do realize that, right?" This decision was hard enough without the added pressure.

Annette held up her hands in defense. "I'm not shaming you. If you feel ashamed, then—"

"I need your support."

Charlene hadn't realized how true it was until she said it out loud. She just wanted her sister to understand where she was coming from. To support her decision. The voice in her head was nasty enough already. She didn't need an external version of it, too.

"I'm being supportive by making sure you're confident in your decision."

"No, you're waiting for me to change my mind."

Annette's nostrils flared. "Because you should—"

"No." Charlene held up a hand to stop her sister. "No, Annette. I know you have an opinion about this, but... this is my choice."

"It's his life, though." Annette hitched a thumb over her shoulder.

"And mine," Charlene said. "It's my life, too. I get a say in this."

"Does Tyler get a say?"

Charlene sighed. "When Margaret was little, she wanted to eat glue and drink from the ocean and run around naked all day. Little kids don't know what's best for them."

"And you do?"

Hardly, she thought. *As my track record proves.* "I'm trying to figure it out. Okay? I know you think I'm rushing into this—throwing Tyler away. But I'm not."

"Sure."

"I'm trying to do what's best for him!"

"What's best for him is to be with his family. It's you."

"Was I what was best for Margaret?" Charlene pinched her lips together the moment she spoke. Like maybe she could draw the words back. Keep them inside.

Annette's expression softened. "Char, that's not—"

Charlene held up a hand to cut her sister off. "I'm the one who has to live with this decision. I'm the one who is responsible for setting the course for Tyler's future. I take that seriously."

"I know you do," Annette said softly.

"I want to do what's best for him."

Annette moved down a step, but kept her arms crossed over her chest. "I know."

"And I'm not sure it's me."

Annette blinked down at her sister. Her face was expressionless. "I don't think we're going to agree on this."

"Probably not," Charlene agreed. "But you don't have to agree with me. You just have to respect me."

Annette narrowed her eyes. "That's a parent-ism if I've ever heard one. You're good."

"I've had a lifetime of practice," Charlene said. "Do you want another one? *Because I said so.*"

"I hated it when Mom said that." Annette laughed begrudgingly. And finally, the tension between them lifted. At least for the span of a moment.

"Is this a truce?" Charlene asked.

Annette nodded. "Truce."

"Good. Because I have big plans today and I wanted you to come."

Twenty minutes later, after Charlene twisted her hair into a low bun and swiped on some blush, then gotten Tyler ready to go, they were all loaded up in the car.

"Where are we going?" Annette finally asked as they crossed the Arthur Ravenel Bridge.

"Brunch," Charlene said, the same kind of way you'd say *Heaven.*

"Thank the Lord. I feel like death," Annette admitted. "I drank too much last night."

"Nothing a breakfast burrito can't fix."

Annette wrinkled her nose. "Pancakes are my hangover cure of choice."

"Cake cakes?" Tyler piped up from the backseat.

Charlene stretched to see him in the rearview mirror. "Do you like pancakes?"

His eyes lit up and he nodded.

"What about fish?" she asked.

He stuck out his tongue.

Charlene laughed. "Not to eat. But to see. Do you like looking at fish?"

His excited squeal was all the answer she needed.

The day passed in a blur of food, fish, and fun. Tyler picked apart his clown pancake at the diner piece by piece. Then, fueled by the sugar, he ran laps around Annette and Charlene at the aquarium.

"Pancakes were a mistake," Annette complained as Tyler dragged her down yet another hallway towards a sea turtle exhibit. "Whipped cream doubly so. I need a nap."

Tyler shook his head violently. "I'm not sleepy!"

And that remained true… until they strapped him into the stroller "Aunt Net" bought for him. Between the sugar crash, the excitement of the morning, and the warm day, he zonked out five minutes into clothes shopping.

"Look at these!" Annette held up a pair of striped overalls with a matching hat. "He could be a little conductor."

"Oh my goodness. Too sweet." Then, Charlene saw the price tag. *Too expensive* was more like it. "I think I saw something similar on the clearance rack. I'll go grab it."

Between clothes and gear and snacks and Pull-Ups, Tyler was quickly becoming pricey. And Jamie had texted just the day before to confirm that the buyers, Chris and Katie, had put in an offer on another house.

Any more buyers you could send my way? Charlene had texted back. She thought about adding a smiley face, but she didn't want to come off as desperate just yet.

No such luck. Sorry. But don't worry. It will sell in no time!

That was the problem: Charlene had no time. She needed the house to be sold yesterday. Last week. Six months ago.

When she swiped her card to pay for the pile of wardrobe basics— plain-colored pocket tees, socks, rocket ship underwear, and elastic shorts—Charlene half-expected it to decline. When it didn't, she said a silent prayer of thanks and all but sprinted out of the store before the cashier could change her mind.

Tyler slept the entire drive back home. But as soon as they pulled into the driveway, he hopped out of the car and set his sights on the beach.

"Let's see turtles," he begged, pointing towards the beach path.

Charlene had never been able to refuse a beach walk. She changed him into the swim trunks and sandals Annette had bought, and they spent the rest of the afternoon splashing in the surf.

It was a perfect day, so long as Charlene didn't focus too long on any of the details. The kind of day she hoped to remember forever.

A moment when things were simple.

Later that night, she woke up to the clumsy turning of her doorknob. A tiny body hopped up onto her bed.

"What do you need, buddy?" Charlene asked in a whisper.

Tyler said nothing as he laid down in what had always been Davy's spot. Even now, five (and a half) years later, Charlene didn't sleep on that side of the bed. It didn't feel right.

"Tyler? What's going on, hon?" she asked.

Her eyes were adjusting to the dark. Charlene could see that Tyler was looking up at her. "Am I gotta leave?"

In many ways, Davy went easy on Margaret. But the one area he'd never budged was letting her sleep in their bed. No matter what bad dream she had or how big the storm raging outside was, Davy always scooped Margaret up and carried her back to her own room.

"You probably should go back to your own bed," she mumbled instead of answering.

"Am I gotta leave?" Tyler repeated. "Or can I stay here?"

Charlene sat up and rubbed a hand on his back. "You should go back to your room, sweetheart."

"No," he whined. He was getting frustrated with her. "Can I stay here or are you gotta give me away?"

Realization washed over Charlene like a bucket of ice water. She gasped. "Oh."

He didn't mean here as in the bed. He meant *here*-here. Here as in home. Here as in with her.

Tyler watched Charlene, on pins and needles waiting for an answer she wasn't ready to give. She wanted to comfort him, but she didn't know how to do that without lying. And she didn't want to lie to him.

Even if he'd one day get over it. Even if he'd one day understand why she did what she did, she couldn't bring herself to do it.

"No one is giving you away," she said gently. "You're just... you're a special boy, and you need a special home."

He furrowed his brow. "A partment?"

"That is a type of home. But I mean, you need a special family."

"Family." He rolled the word around in his mouth a few times.

"Like Mommy—she was your family. And so am I. And Aunt Net."

Charlene could practically see the gears turning in his head. Could see him trying to wrap his little mind around the concept. When he finally looked up at her, his eyes were glassy. "Where is Mommy?"

Yet another question Charlene didn't have an answer for. Not a good one, at least.

So instead, she slid over to Davy's side of the bed and tucked Tyler into her arms. She held him against her chest and hummed a wordless song to him until he fell asleep.

After a little while, the raw edges of her own heart didn't ache quite as badly as they always did.

~

THE NEXT DAY AT SAFE HARBOR ADOPTION AGENCY

Noah was right about Safe Harbor Adoption Agency being faster than the DSS. One phone call early that morning had Charlene penciled in for a midday meeting with a caseworker named Felicia. If nothing else went right, Charlene could at least say they were efficient.

"Miss Wilson?" A woman in a dark skirt and pale pink button down smiled at Charlene across a modern lobby. "I'm Felicia. I'm ready if you are."

Charlene was ready, too. More ready than she'd been for her meeting with Noah. Her hair was dry, she had make-up on, and her dark gray trousers and white flowy top gave her a put-together finish. Felicia, at least, couldn't judge her appearance.

They went down a well-lit hallway with professional photos of smiling babies and happy families hanging from the walls. When Felicia directed Charlene into a small office and shut the door, the ambient sound from the hallway disappeared. Charlene was grateful for the privacy.

"You provided a few details over the phone." Felicia plucked a piece of paper off a stack next to her and skimmed it. "I'd just like to verify those. Your grandson is three?"

"I believe," Charlene said. "I'm not in contact with his mom, so I'm not entirely sure when he was born."

"Because she reached out to a judge, we do have a contact number for her. If there's anything you can't answer, then we can call her for more details."

Charlene bit back her desire to ask for Margaret's number. She knew they probably wouldn't give it to her. But what she wouldn't do to be able to call Margaret and... well, she didn't know what. Give her a piece of her mind? Ask for an explanation? Simply hear her daughter's voice?

Charlene's throat thickened with emotion. She swallowed it back. "Okay, great."

"And since Margaret has expressed interest in severing her rights, that makes this process much easier," Felicia continued. "We would need to wait until a judge handed down a decision, but after that, we have a waitlist of families."

You're a special boy, and you need a special home. Her words to Tyler played in her head like a constant refrain.

"I assume there is some kind of vetting process?"

"Absolutely." Felicia grabbed a pamphlet from a wire bin on the corner of her desk and slid it across the desk. "This outlines our entire process. It is quite thorough. Our job is to place children in their forever homes with their forever families. We do not take that lightly. Even after the placement has been made, our agents will follow up with the family at one month, six months, and one year intervals to check on their progress and be sure everyone is settling in well. And we remain a resource to our families for life."

Charlene scanned the pamphlet without really seeing it. She was still so stunned to be sitting in the room that her brain was having a hard time processing anything else. "That sounds... nice."

Clinical was actually the word at the forefront of Charlene's mind.

Felicia leaned forward slightly and lowered her chin. Her smile was kind. "I know the decision you are making is a big one. Unimaginably so. But if I can try to offer some comfort, I'll say that we don't place a child with a family unless we are certain they are a good fit. Actually, I just spoke with a couple today who have been working with us for two years."

"They've been trying to adopt for two years?" Charlene asked.

"They are a wonderful couple, but we haven't found the right kiddo for them yet. There are some agencies that will simply pair a child with anyone who walks through the door, but we do things differently here," Felicia said. "And we take your opinion into consideration."

"How so?"

"Well, whether you want a closed or open adoption is one significant decision you'll make."

"Open or closed, as in…?"

"Whether or not you have continued contact with Tyler or not," Felicia explained. "If you'd like to stay in his life, then we would need to place him with a family who are willing to allow that."

"And if I choose a closed adoption, then I won't see him again?"

"Not unless he makes attempts to find you. Which, with DNA websites and social media, is happening more and more every day. But nothing is promised, and he would have to come to you."

Can I stay here or are you gotta give me away?

How much worse would that question sting when it came from a grown Tyler? Right now, he was a little boy. He couldn't fully understand what was happening. But what would happen when he did understand?

What if he came to hate her? To blame her?

What if she made the wrong choice?

Charlene's chest tightened. Sitting in this tidy, soundproof office, she felt more overwhelmed than she had in the midst of the noise hurricane that was the DSS building.

"We want you to feel comfortable with the placement because we aren't just taking care of Tyler," added Felicia. "We're taking care of you, too."

All Charlene could do was nod. Her throat had closed up. Was she having an allergic reaction? It had never happened before, but there was a first time for everything.

Charlene was about to signal for some water or a fan, but before she could, Felicia's cell phone rang.

"Sorry, I usually put this on silent when I'm—" She looked up at Charlene and winced. "I'm sorry, but would you mind if I took this?"

Charlene waved her on. Felicia thanked her and stepped into the hallway.

Immediately, Charlene could breathe a little easier. What was happening to her? This is what she'd wanted, right? Tyler gone as soon as possible. Tyler taken care of? Just rip the Band-Aid off. But now, even thinking the words felt dirty.

Safe Harbor Adoption Agency was lovely. Everything anyone wanting to adopt a child could hope for. So why did Charlene feel like the walls were closing in on her?

Before she could second-guess herself, Charlene grabbed her purse, stood up, and walked to the door. She turned the knob and peeked out through a crack in the door.

The hallway was clear. No Felicia in sight.

Charlene let out a sigh of a relief and bolted. There was no need to bolt, strictly speaking. She wasn't a prisoner being held hostage. She wasn't under arrest. She could leave whenever she wanted.

But if Charlene had to talk to someone about how she was feeling and why she wanted to leave, she was certain her words would end up splattered on their shoes instead. So, following the path she'd walked just fifteen minutes earlier, Charlene retreated down the hallway, crossed the lobby without looking at the receptionist, and stepped back into the warm sunlight She didn't stop until she was in her car and the doors were locked.

Then she dropped her forehead onto the hot steering wheel and cried.

9

AFTERNOON AT CHARLENE'S HOUSE

The drive home from Safe Harbor did a lot to calm Charlene down. The more miles she put between herself and Felicia, the more at peace she felt. Still, when she made it home, she was distracted. She could feel Annette watching her closely all afternoon.

Charlene hadn't told her sister about the meeting with the adoption agency. Annette likely suspected something was amiss, though. Where else would Charlene need to rush off to in the middle of the day?

"You're quiet," Annette said when she came downstairs. She'd volunteered to put Tyler down for a nap and Charlene had readily agreed.

"I don't have much to say today."

"I know. Under different circumstances, I'd be grateful. But as it is…"

Charlene forced her face into a smile. "Rude."

Annette dropped down next to her on the couch and nudged her in the rib. "Come on. Tell Annette all your problems."

Well, that list would be far too long for one conversation. So Charlene decided to go with the most pressing problem.

"I had a meeting with an adoption agency. Safe Harbor."

Annette groaned. "Cheesy name."

"Says the creator of the Wilson Wonders.'" Charlene took a deep breath. "It was really nice. They have a solid vetting process… I think. I actually haven't read the pamphlet yet."

"Sounds like you've done your research."

Charlene wanted to be offended, but when she looked over, Annette was smirking at her. Teasing. It seemed they really were in a truce.

"They take their jobs really seriously. I'd trust them to place kids with the right families."

"So then what's the problem?" she asked.

Charlene couldn't answer. Because she didn't have an answer. Or maybe she did.

She trusted Safe Harbor to do their job well when it came to other kids. But Tyler wasn't just another kid. He was her grandson.

"You need to get out of the house," Annette said all at once. She stood up and held a hand out to Charlene. "Go for a walk or—*oh*, go for a bike ride! Change it up. Get out of your own head."

Charlene shook her head. "I don't want to go for a bike ride. I feel exhausted."

"Even more of a sign you need to get up and go. Trust me."

"But what about Tyler? He's going to wake up and—"

"And Aunt Net will be here to take care of him," she said. "I can handle it."

Charlene stumbled towards the garage door as Annette pushed her from behind. "I don't even know if I can still ride a bike. It has been... oh, jeez, it's been twenty years, probably."

Annette laughed. "You'll be fine. They don't say 'it's like riding a bike' for nothing. You never forget."

Just as Annette reached around Charlene to open the door and officially shove her out, Charlene skidded to a stop. "Okay, fine. I'll go! But can I at least change first?"

"Oh." Annette scanned her outfit. "Slacks and a button-down aren't great workout clothes. Fine. I'll allow it."

"Thank you."

Charlene slipped into a pair of navy-blue leggings, a loose white tank top, and a pair of slip-on white shoes. As soon as she was ready, Annette picked up right where she'd left off by pushing Charlene into the garage.

"I'll be back in an hour."

"No rush," Annette said. "Take a long ride. Grab yourself a drink. Maybe even some dinner. I'll hold down the fort."

It had never been in Charlene's nature to ask for help. But mostly because she'd never had to ask Davy for much help. He'd just helped, simple as that. It wasn't until Annette was offering to "hold down the fort" that Charlene realized how much she'd been taking on the last five years.

Maybe it would be nice to walk away for a minute. To do something for herself.

"Fine," she relented, slinging her leg over the bike. "Tell Tyler I'll be back later, okay?"

"Sure, sure. Go on. Get!"

Charlene laughed and peddled away. After one quick wobble, she got things on the right track and sailed off down the road.

Annette was right: riding a bike was just like riding a bike.

But muscles Charlene didn't even know she had burned as she zipped off along the backroads. She snaked down 34th Avenue towards Forest Trail, then rode Waterway Boulevard so she could peek through the trees at the marsh beyond.

After a while, the burn in her arms and legs began to fade. Charlene started to feel good. Surprisingly good. It felt cheesy even to think it, so she'd never say as much to Annette, but Charlene felt like she was flying. Which is probably why she didn't consciously realize she was on the complete opposite side of the Isle of Palms until she saw signs for Front Beach.

She hadn't intended to take Annette up on her offer of staying out for a drink, but the thought of turning around and immediately riding all the way back home was daunting. Plus, she was parched. Which is how she found herself leaning her bike against the railing of Luke 'n Ollie's Pizzeria and grabbing a table on the patio.

"Can I interest you in a cocktail or anything from the bar?" the waitress asked.

"Better just make it an iced tea," Charlene said. The memory of the previous day's hangover was still too fresh.

A couple with a little girl close to Tyler's age were sitting two tables over. The dad was leaned back nursing a beer while the mom tried to convince the little girl to try a cucumber.

"If you don't like it, you can eat a bite of cheese pizza to wash it down," she said. "But I think you'll like it. Especially with ranch dressing."

The little girl crossed her arms and screwed up her face in disgust. "Yucky."

"If you eat it, I'll let you have ice cream," the dad said.

Immediately, the mom gave him a warning look. "No bribery."

But it was too late. The little girl snatched the cucumber out of her mom's hand and shoved it into her mouth. As soon as she swallowed, she threw her chubby arms up in victory. "Ice cream!"

"Great," the woman groaned. "Look what you've done."

Charlene couldn't help but smile. It was like going back in time to when Margaret was little. The way Charlene would barter and beg Margaret to be reasonable, to make compromises. And then Davy would swoop in at the last minute and be the hero. It had driven her crazy to no end back then. But time had a way of turning even the most frustrating moments into fond memories.

Noah's advice the day before had felt useless. *You'll always regret what you don't do.* It was useless. That hadn't stopped Charlene from rolling it over in her head again and again since the moment she shut the door on him.

Would she regret giving Tyler up? After everything Charlene had been through with Margaret, she should regret ever deciding to have a child in the first place. But of course she didn't.

She could never regret her daughter.

So even if raising Tyler turned into as much of a disaster as raising Margaret had, would Charlene ever regret it? She didn't think so.

But could she do that to Tyler? Could she risk his future for her own selfish reasons? That, she wasn't so sure of.

The family packed up their things and left a few minutes later, headed in the direction of the ice cream shop down the street. Charlene still felt as exhausted as she'd been when she sat down. But if she was going to make it home before it got too dark, she needed to get a move on, too.

Charlene slung her already sore leg over the bike and headed home. Whatever mental barrier she'd managed to break through earlier, it was impenetrable this time around. She was exhausted, plain and simple. At what she estimated to be the halfway mark, her calf muscle suddenly began to seize.

Charlene tried to push through the tightness, but her leg grew stiffer with each passing second. Pain shot up her leg, practically paralyzing her hip. Clumsily, she pulled off into a patch of grass and hobbled off the bike.

"Ow, ow," she whimpered. She pointed and flexed her foot to ease the knot building in her calf. Even as the pain began to ebb, she could tell her muscle would be sore in the morning. Annette would get an earful about this.

Charlene heard a car coming and turned around to see a white pickup truck pulling up along the side of Palm Boulevard behind her.

She smiled and politely waved the person on. The truck shuddered as the driver shifted it into park. Charlene waved them along more frantically and shook her head.

"I'm fine," she called. "Thanks, but I'm okay. Go ahead and—"

The driver's door opened and a familiar head of salt and pepper hair climbed down out of the truck.

"… Noah."

He grinned at her. "Fancy running into you here."

"I'd say I'm surprised, but at this point, I should just expect to see you when I turn around."

"You make me sound like a stalker," he teased.

She shrugged. "If it looks like a duck and sounds like a—"

"I'm not a duck. Or a stalker." He pointed to the far corner of the island. "I'm headed to the marina. But I noticed a biker in distress and had to stop."

"Of course you did."

"I'm kind that way." He smirked and then ran an appraising eye down her leg. "Cramp?"

"A small one, very minor," she lied. "It's gone now. I should actually get going again before it gets dark."

"You have a couple hours until sunset."

"Well, my sister is home alone with Tyler. I'm sure she—"

"Will manage fine on her own while you come out with me on my boat?" he finished for her. "Don't make me beg. It'll be fun."

Charlene let out a surprised laugh. "That was subtle."

"To be honest, subtlety has never been my flavor."

Charlene's cheeks betrayed her by blushing. "I'm not sure if that would be such a good idea."

"Who said anything about it being a good idea?" he asked. "I said it would be fun. I find they tend to be inversely correlated, actually."

His expression was all innocence, but his eyes told a very different story. Yesterday morning at her house, he'd been all business. Or mostly business, anyway. Charlene couldn't helping being curious what he was like outside of work hours.

She pursed her lips. "Fine."

"Great." Noah smiled and crossed the distance between them in a few strides. He grabbed her bike and started wheeling it towards his truck.

"But only if you drive me home afterward. In the interest of honesty, that cramp wasn't so minor after all."

Noah nodded like that was a given. "What kind of date would I be if I didn't drive you home?"

"This isn't a date."

He looked back over his shoulder and winked. "Whatever you say."

Instantly, Charlene knew her first instinct had been right. This was not a good idea. Curiosity alone was not a good enough reason to be doing this. He was Tyler's caseworker, for goodness' sake. It was inappropriate.

Or… maybe it wasn't. She wasn't familiar with the etiquette around this kind of thing. Even if she was, she doubted it would matter. She had no interest in hitting the brakes now.

As soon as Noah pulled his boat away from the marina and headed out on the water, Charlene had to admit it sure looked like a date. *And if it looks like a date and sounds like a date…*

It wasn't, of course. But she could see how someone might be confused.

Before they got on board, Noah stopped into the marina for snacks to pair with the beer he already had in his cooler. "I would have brought wine if I'd known I was going to have company," he said. "But you're welcome to anything in the cooler."

"Just water is fine with me." Charlene grabbed a water bottle and dried off the outside with the hem of her shirt. Noah had already seen her overindulge with alcohol once. No need for a repeat.

The boat was bright red and sixteen feet long, according to Noah. From the dock, it had looked plenty big. Now that they were skimming across the water, the shore behind growing smaller and smaller, Charlene felt like they might as well be on a single jet ski.

There was nowhere to escape. Unless Charlene wanted to turn her bike ride into a triathlon and swim back to shore, she was stuck in Noah's boat until he decided to return her ashore.

"Do you have a boat?" Noah asked as he eased off the throttle. They slowed to a casual coast, slicing quietly across the glassy waters of the Intracoastal Waterway as herons winged over the marsh grasses on either side of them.

"Do kayaks count?"

Noah laughed. "Technically, I suppose. But that's like saying you have a golf cart when someone asks if you have a car."

"We used to have a golf cart!"

Noah killed the engine and let the boat drift on its own. He spun around in the driver's seat to look at her. "We?"

"My husband and I," Charlene explained. "Late husband. He died five years ago. Five and a half years, if you want to get technical."

Noah's brow furrowed, and Charlene could see realization dawn. "Oh."

"Yeah. Right before my daughter ran away," she admitted.

"I'm so sorry."

Few people knew the details with Margaret. Even Annette hadn't known it all until recently. Charlene had carried these things alone for so long. It felt nice to open up to someone. She was also aware this was Noah's job. Or adjacent to his job, anyway.

"She didn't handle it so great. And we never got along especially well, anyway." Charlene waved a hand dismissively. "But that's an old, sad story. I don't need to get into it."

Noah stood up and began sorting through his fishing supplies. "By all means, get into it. I don't mind."

"I don't want you to feel like you're working."

He held his arms out, turning in a half-circle. "It's impossible to feel like I'm working when I'm out here," he said. "This boat is my meditation. It's where I come to relax."

"Even more reason for me to spare you my sob story."

He shook his head. "I want you to feel relaxed, too. This may not be a date, according to you, but I'd like you to be comfortable."

"I am," Charlene said, surprising even herself with how much she meant it.

Opening up to people—getting close—had never come easily to her. But Noah made it feel natural. Somehow, the rude man from the DSS office had become someone she actually enjoyed spending time with.

Noah held out a fishing pole to her and grinned. "Good."

Charlene leaned back and shook her head. "Maybe not that comfortable."

"Wait, what?" He tilted his head to the side. "You don't like to fish?"

She shrugged. "Don't like to, don't know how to. To-may-toe, to-mah-toe."

Noah's eyes widened in horror. "How long have you lived on the island?"

"Forty-five years."

He pressed a hand to his heart. "You're telling me you've lived on this island your entire life, but you don't know how to fish?"

"It's not that shocking."

"I'm not shocked—I'm horrified. You have to let me teach you."

Davy had gone fishing with his friends more weekends than not during their marriage. But they spent so much time with each other already, since they worked and lived together, that Charlene thought it was best she let Davy have his own hobbies. After all, he didn't join her when she went thrifting or to get a manicure.

It wasn't that she didn't want to learn. It was just that she'd never had the cause. Or the opportunity. Now, she had both.

Noah wanted to teach her. And Charlene had a feeling it would make him happy if she let him. For reasons she didn't yet understand, she wanted to make him happy.

"Fine," she relented. "But you can't wrap your arms around me and pretend you're helping me with my form. I've seen that move, I've scouted that move, and I'm here to warn you that that move is strictly off-limits."

"Too right you are." He sighed, a smirk creeping across his face. "Fine. Agreed. I can't guarantee I'll be able to teach you properly without that all-important step, but..." He held up both hands as if in surrender, "I'm hands-off if you wish."

"Good. Thank you."

"Don't thank me yet," he said. "It's very likely you won't catch a single thing."

Charlene retreated to the opposite side of the boat. She bit back a smile. "That's a risk I'm willing to take."

10

EVENING AT THE MARINA

"I cannot believe you caught a fish and I didn't." Noah shook his head as he secured his boat to the dock. "I just… I can't believe it."

Charlene held up the ten-gallon bucket containing her spotted trout. "Believe it. The student has become the master."

Noah snorted. "Hardly. Don't forget who had to reel it in the last ten feet. You nearly lost it."

"Because you were bouncing around behind me and nearly knocked me off the boat!"

He waved her off with a disgruntled mumble, but when Charlene caught his eye, he grinned. He was proud, even if he wouldn't admit it.

When he finished with the boat, Noah straightened up and planted his hands on his hips. "Well, the only thing left to do is to let me clean and cook that fish for you."

"That's the *only* thing to do?" Charlene asked. "It seems like calling it a night and going home is an option, too."

"Robbing a bank also remains on the table. Are you game?"

Charlene rolled her eyes, but she had to admit she was starving. After visiting the adoption agency that morning, she hadn't been overly hungry for lunch. Now, between the bike ride and the fishing, her body was running on empty. She needed nutrients. Plus, she was in no position to turn down a free meal, what with her finances being the mess that they were.

"Fine. Okay," she said.

Noah immediately shook his head. "Hold your horses. This is the third time I've brought up a fun, exciting new idea and the third time you've acted like you're doing me a favor. *Fine* isn't good enough."

"What do you want me to say?"

He batted his lashes and said in an obnoxious, high-pitched voice, "*Oh Noah, that sounds wonderful. Thank you ever-so-much for the invitation. I'd be delighted.*"

Charlene crossed her arms. "In your dreams, pal."

"Okay, then at least admit you want to come over for dinner," he said. "I know I may come off confident and smooth, but I have my pride, Charlene."

Mischief sparked in his eyes. Noah was dangerous. Charlene had only spent a few hours with him, but it was obvious. How he was still single was anybody's guess. How Charlene was supposed to resist his charms was also anybody's guess. She certainly didn't have the answers.

"Yes, Noah," she mumbled. "I want to come over for dinner."

His face split into a wide smile. "Then let's go."

Noah lived much closer to Charlene than she expected. For a moment as he'd driven from the marina towards his house, Charlene had thought he was taking her back to her home. That forcing her to admit she wanted to have dinner with him was just some cruel prank before he'd take her home and dump her and her bike in the front lawn with a goodbye and a see-you-never.

But then he'd turned off on a side road and parked in front of a little blue bungalow. Palm trees ran along the curb and well-manicured bushes framed the walkway. It was a cute house.

Rather than walk up the front, however, Noah led Charlene straight around the side of the house to the backyard. He unlocked his garage and immediately got to work on the fish, scraping and cleaning and deboning.

Once that was taken care of, he went to a refrigerator at the back of the garage and pulled out a marinade that he slathered over the meat.

"Do you have a kitchen inside?" Charlene asked.

Noah chuckled. "Yeah, but I like doing the fish prep out here. It's easier clean-up. I can just scoop the scraps into the trash and hose everything else off."

"So you do this often then?"

"Cook fish or go fishing?" he asked. "Actually, it doesn't matter. The answer is 'yes' to both."

"It's nice you have a hobby."

The fish was slathered in marinade now. Noah waved for Charlene to follow him across his back patio and into the kitchen. "Yeah, I suppose. But doesn't everybody?"

Charlene thought about it. "I'm not sure I do."

Noah flipped on the kitchen light with his elbow and seamlessly grabbed a stainless-steel pan from where it hung from a hook on the wall. He slid it onto the stove and started pre-heating it. "Excuse me?"

"Flipping houses was my hobby," she explained. "Then it became my job. I used to go thrifting, but even that was usually for staging houses."

"So you really don't have any hobbies?" He pressed. "Nothing?"

Charlene shrugged. "Not anymore."

"What changed?" He crossed his arms and leaned back against the countertop.

His kitchen wasn't especially modern or up-to-date, but it had a nice hominess. Well-loved cookware hung from rows of hooks on the walls. He had fish-shaped glass canisters that held flour and sugar next to a copper tea kettle on the counter.

It was obvious to Charlene that Noah was a man perfectly at ease with himself. His personality and his sense of design said as much. Charlene found it a little disarming, if she was being honest. But two could play that game.

"My husband died," she said flatly. "And my daughter ran off."

Noah pursed his lips. "Yep. That'll do it."

"Once they were gone, it felt silly to take time for myself. I was alone all the time already. What did I need more time for myself for?"

Not once in the last five and a half years had Charlene stopped to wonder why she didn't go out for a Saturday morning coffee and pastry anymore. Or why her golf clubs had done nothing but gather dust since Davy's diagnosis. Aside from her daily beach walk, Charlene woke up, went to work, and went to sleep. There wasn't much excitement.

Until recently.

"You were out for a bike ride when I found you today," Noah said. "Is that a hobby?"

She shook her head. "Absolutely not. Annette forced me into it. She said I needed to get out of the house. Clear my head."

"You seem clear-headed right now. Did it work?" Noah held his hand over the pan on the stove for a minute. He must have determined it was hot enough because he squeezed in some oil and then dumped the fish into the pan. It began to splatter and sizzle immediately.

"Maybe. I might also just be distracted."

He grinned at her over his shoulder. "A good kind of distracted?"

She rolled her eyes. "Now, you're fishing for compliments."

"A man has to try. Lord knows that fishing for fish didn't work out today."

They both chuckled as the fish seared in the pan. "Yes," she finally admitted. "It was a good kind of distraction. This morning, I went to the adoption agency you recommended. It left me a little flustered."

His smile shifted to an expression of concern. "You didn't like it?"

"No, no. It's not that. It seemed great. It's just…" Charlene didn't even know how to finish that sentence. "I left in the middle of the meeting when the caseworker was out of the room."

"Oh. Well, sounds not so great, all things considered."

"Yeah. I just couldn't do it. She was talking about closed or open adoptions and caring about my opinion, and…" Charlene sighed. "Tyler asked me last night if I was going to get rid of him."

Noah nodded slowly as he moved the fish around the pan, letting the pieces brown. "What did you say?"

"Nothing really. I didn't know what to say."

"You didn't know or you didn't want to say?" he asked.

Charlene narrowed her eyes playfully. "Stop being so insightful. It's making it hard to clear my head."

He smiled. "Sorry. But you have to find the answers to these questions eventually."

"Am I talking to Caseworker Noah right now?"

"How about you're talking to your friend Noah?" he suggested.

Charlene bobbed her head and then jumped up to sit on the edge of the counter. "Okay. Sure. I like that."

"Great. And Friend Noah wants to know how you're feeling about your grandson living with you."

She weighed her answer. Things had been going better with Tyler than Charlene had expected. The longer he lived with her, the more at ease he became. He was starting to talk more. He wasn't afraid to let Charlene and Annette know he didn't like the steamed broccoli they served him for dinner. And he'd finally started going upstairs to use the bathroom on his own. He was making himself at home. Charlene loved to see it.

"I never thought I'd have another little kid in my house," she murmured. "I was young when I had Margaret. Davy and I were busy building our business. I didn't get to devote as much time to her as I always imagined I would."

"But things are different with Tyler now?"

She nodded. "They could be. They feel different."

"Good different, bad different, or just different different?"

Charlene's shoulders sagged. "These are hard questions."

"Sorry," he laughed. "I don't mean to put you on the spot, but—"

"No, it's fine. I need to think about these things."

Annette had tried pushing Charlene into a decision, guilting her into keeping Tyler. But Charlene had never willingly been pushed into anything. Davy used to joke that you could lead some horses to water but you couldn't make them drink. "But I can't even lead you to water," he'd always say with a laugh. "You'd sooner die of thirst than let me lead you anywhere."

This decision, whatever she decided, needed to be Charlene's and Charlene's alone.

It didn't matter that Tyler's hazel eyes melted her heart. Or that her first thought when she woke up in the morning was for him and what they'd do that day. It didn't matter that, even as she spoke with caseworkers and adoption agencies, Charlene was already mentally planning out a fall trip to a pumpkin patch and a Halloween costume for the little one.

Finally, she nodded. "Tyler makes things good different. Really good."

Noah flicked off the burner and gave the fish one more turn. The pieces were golden brown now. The marinade had caramelized deliciously, and Charlene's mouth watered.

"So what does that mean?" he asked.

The answer sat in her chest, fully formed. But it took her a minute to be able to say it out loud. She cleared her throat and took a deep breath. "Well, I guess it means... it means I want Tyler to stay with me."

She did. She really did.

"Charlene, that's—I'm really happy for you," Noah said. His eyes glimmered. "This is the best-case scenario from my perspective. It's the kind of outcome we hope for."

He was looking at her so warmly that Charlene felt jittery. She slid off the counter and looked down at her shoes. "Um, thanks."

"Anyone with eyes can see that Tyler will be in good hands with you," he continued. "I didn't doubt it from the moment I saw you walk into DSS with him. There was something about you that just—"

Charlene's heart began to race. She'd just made a big decision. That was enough excitement for one day. There was no need for... whatever Noah was doing.

"Smells good," she said, interrupting him.

Charlene stepped forward and reached around Noah to pluck a piece of fish from the pan. It was hot and she popped it into her mouth quickly to save her fingers.

As she did, Noah stepped forward, too. Before Charlene could do anything about it, they were standing chest to chest. Then, to her surprise, Noah wrapped his arms around her. It was a hug. Just a hug —but a warm, friendly, cologne- and saltwater-scented hug that overwhelmed her in every way possible.

Charlene inhaled sharply in surprise, which was exactly the wrong thing to do. The piece of hot fish shot to the back of her throat and lodged there. Charlene wheezed, but that only seemed to make things worse. She couldn't breathe at all.

She stumbled back from Noah and tried to fill her lungs to cough, but nothing was coming in or out. Her windpipe was completely closed.

"Charlene, are you—?" Noah's brow furrowed in concern and then shot up, practically disappearing in his salt and pepper hair. "Are you choking?"

Choking? No, she wasn't choking. She could get this out. She just needed a good hit to shake things up and—

Charlene pounded a fist against her chest, but nothing happened. Her vision was starting to go black on the edges. This was it. This is how she would die.

"Charlene, you're choking." It was a statement rather than a question this time. "I'm going to give you the Heimlich Maneuver, okay?"

There wasn't time to argue or nod or think about it at all. One second, Charlene was blacking out in the middle of Noah's kitchen. The next, his arms were around her, her back was pressed to his front, and he was thrusting his closed fists up into her gut.

Charlene felt like a rag doll being shaken by a violent dog. But after the third blow came sweet relief. The fish dislodged from her windpipe and shot out of her mouth. It splattered against the window in Noah's back door. A filmy streak of marinade and spit was left behind as it dropped to the floor.

She gasped for air as Noah rubbed her back. "Are you okay?" he asked. "Do you need some water?"

She shook her head. *Air.* She just needed air.

But as air once again filled her lungs and oxygenated her brain, Charlene regained the ability to process how horrifically embarrassing the last ninety seconds were. She almost wished she'd passed out. At least it would have spared her this moment.

Noah stepped closer to her and wrapped an arm around her shoulders. He chuckled. "That was terrifying."

The kitchen smelled like fish and lemon juice, but Noah smelled like the sea. Like salt and a warm breeze. He was charming and handsome and smelled good...

And Charlene had just choked on a bite of fish right in front of him like a dog scarfing its dinner down too fast.

"I'm fine." She quickly stepped out of his arms. "Totally fine. I don't know what happened."

"You choked," he said. "It was probably my fault. I thought you were coming in for a hug, and I squeezed as you were eating, and—"

The last thing she needed was a play-by-play. "I'm fine!" she practically screeched. "Totally fine. But it is getting late. My sister doesn't know where I am. I should be home to help put Tyler to bed."

Noah frowned. "You don't have to go. We haven't even eaten yet. You can stay and—"

Absolutely not. Charlene was marinating in an embarrassment stew and she was positive that she'd drown if she didn't get out.

"I'm not even hungry anymore. Almost dying will do that to you." She laughed, though nothing at all was funny. "Really, I'll just go and—"

"Charlene, please stay," Noah said. "I'm sorry if I crossed a line or made you uncomfortable. I just—"

"I'm not uncomfortable," she lied. "You didn't do anything. You saved my life, so thanks. And now I have to go. Home."

Noah's shoulders sagged, but he nodded. "Okay, I'll grab my keys and I can drive—"

"I'll ride my bike. I live close by," she explained. "But I guess you already know that. Since you've been there."

"You shouldn't be riding. It's dark and you just choked. I want to make sure you get home okay."

"I'll be fine." Charlene backed towards the door and waved. "Thanks for the boat. And the fishing. And the one bite of fish. It was delicious. For a second. Anyway, goodbye."

Her face was flaming as Charlene hurtled across Noah's deck to where his truck was parked in the driveway. She struggled getting her bike out of the bed of his pickup. But the moment the wheels were on the driveway, she threw her leg over the seat and peddled away as fast as humanly possible.

11

EVENING AT CHARLENE'S HOUSE

When Charlene made it home, her chest hurt, both from having received the Heimlich less than a half hour earlier and from the bike ride. But the tightness eased when she turned up her driveway and saw a little boy running around her yard in a fit of giggles.

Fireflies danced and flickered just out of his reach, but Tyler wasn't discouraged. He had the kind of undimming optimism only little kids can have. The kind Charlene desperately hoped would rub off on her.

"Back already?" Annette called from the porch. She was in a pair of cut off jean shorts and a t-shirt. She looked right at home.

"I've been gone for five hours."

"Grandma!" Tyler buried his face against her leg for a second before he ran back into the yard. "I'm hunting lightning bugs."

"And he's doing great. He has caught three already." Annette held up a mason jar with a few bugs flickering behind the glass.

"I wanna catch a lot!"

"You go for it, bud. We'll watch you from right here." Charlene dropped down gratefully onto the brick steps. Her joints sighed in relief.

"Hard ride?"

Charlene chuckled. "Can you tell?"

"You look both pale and flushed, somehow," Annette said. "And you smell."

"Oh gosh, do I?" Charlene dipped her nose close to her armpit and groaned. "Well, that's embarrassing."

"It's just me. I shared a room with you for almost two decades, remember? I had a front row seat to your morning breath every day."

Charlene waved her sister away. "I don't care about you. What's embarrassing is that you aren't the only one who smelled me."

"Who else would be so bold?"

A week ago, this was the kind of thing Charlene would have kept to herself. No need to relive the trauma. But now, she liked having someone to talk with. Someone to process things with. Back before everything—even before Davy—Annette was her someone. It was nice to have her back.

"You remember the DSS worker?"

Annette gasped. "Handsome Noah?"

"Is that what you're calling him?"

"It's what everyone should call him," Annette teased. "That man is outdoors catalog handsome. He could sell overpriced sweaters to me any day."

Charlene laughed. "Well, he picked me up on the side of the road. Going for a bike ride didn't clear my head so much as it left me crippled."

"You look fine to me. Did something happen?"

"Noah found me cramping."

"He just *found* you?"

"Completely random," Charlene confirmed. "He swears he isn't stalking me, at least. So I think it's completely random."

"Even if he was stalking you…" Annette shrugged like it was no big deal.

"Then he asked me to go fishing with him."

Annette was on the edge of the step now, eyes wide. "Like, on a date? When? I'll watch Tyler whenever you need. You have to go!"

"I already did." Charlene bit back a smile. After the way Annette had gone on about "Handsome Noah," she liked being able to lay a small claim on him—even though he was not hers to claim, and she definitely did not want him to be. "He was headed to the marina, and he asked me to come. So… I did."

"Woot! Woot!" Annette gave an embarrassing fist pump. "Look at you go! I'm so proud of you. That's a huge step."

"Don't be so proud. It was not a date. And even if it had been, it didn't end super well."

"Oh no. What did he do?"

"He hugged me."

"How dare he?!" Annette crowed in faux rage. "The sheer nerve on men these days! Why, they think they can just—"

"The hug was fine."

That much was honest. The bike ride home had provided Charlene with ten minutes of uninterrupted time to think about the warm, cologne-infused hug Noah had given her. And how, for a brief second before the fish lodged in her windpipe, it had been more than fine. It had been really... nice.

"What's the problem, then? Are you upset that a hug is all he gave you?" Annette wagged her brows.

"No. Because that isn't all he did. He also saved my life." A new flood of embarrassment washed over Charlene. At least this time she could almost laugh about it. She dropped her head in her hands and fought a bitter laugh. "I choked on a piece of fish. He had to give me the Heimlich."

Annette clapped a hand over her mouth. "You're kidding!"

"I wish I was."

"You choked? Choked *choked?*"

Charlene sighed. "I full-on choked. It was a couldn't-breathe, windpipe-closed-shut kind of choking. I was starting to black out."

"But you're okay now?" Annette ran a hand down Charlene's arm like she was checking her for outward signs of damage.

"Oh yeah, I'm fine. Noah took care of it in a couple seconds, but... it was humiliating."

"It really is."

"Gee, thanks," Charlene snorted.

"Do you want me to lie?" Annette asked. "It *is* embarrassing. But at least you're alive. And now you know Noah is good under pressure."

"Yeah, but now I know I'm not."

Annette frowned. "What does that mean?"

"I ran away as soon as I could breathe. I felt like I was going to die of embarrassment." Charlene shook her head. "He probably thinks I'm deranged. I thought him seeing me hungover the other morning was the worst, but I keep hitting new personal lows in front of him."

"Come on, I'm sure it's not that bad."

"It's definitely that bad."

"Negative Nancy." Annette nudged her arm. "Let's recalibrate. Did anything good happen on your date?"

"It wasn't a date," Charlene said again quickly. "Let me think. I guess it wasn't all bad. I did make a pretty big decision about—"

Charlene's answer was interrupted by Tyler's squeal as he ran towards them, hands cupped together. "Aunt Net, I got one!"

Annette hurried and opened the jar a crack so the other fireflies wouldn't escape as Tyler tipped the one in his hands inside. Once the lid was closed, he admired his haul through the glass. After a few seconds of awe, it was back to hunting.

Charlene smiled. "I made a pretty big decision."

"Oh?" Annette set the mason jar on the step next to her. "About?"

Charlene gestured towards where Tyler was standing in the grass. His head was tipped back as far as it could go. Fireflies glimmered in the air around him like stars. "The little one."

Annette went still. "Oh. Okay."

"It's good." Charlene turned towards her sister, emotion gathering in her eyes. "Really good."

"How good?"

Charlene swallowed. "I think I want to—I *know* I want to keep him. I want to adopt him."

She could barely get the sentence out before Annette threw her arms around her neck and squeezed. "Oh, Char! You won't regret it. I know you won't. This will be the best decision you ever make. He is so happy here, and you are going to be so happy together. Everyone is going to be so happy."

"If we make it that far," Charlene wheezed, trying to pry Annette's arm from around her neck. "I'm going to choke for the second time tonight unless you let go."

Annette dropped her arms and laughed. "Sorry. I'm just... I'm so happy. He's such a sweet kid, Char."

Suddenly, Tyler was waving both arms over his head at someone coming down the sidewalk. It was too dark for Charlene to see who it was, but Tyler was excited.

"Hello!"

A woman laughed and Charlene knew immediately it was Elaine. "Hi there, Mr. Tyler! I was hoping you'd still be here."

"I'm hunting lightning bugs." Midway through the sentence, Tyler spun in a circle to lunge at a firefly that buzzed by his head.

"How fun!" Elaine tousled his hair as she passed and then waved towards the porch. "How are you two this fine evening?"

"Amazing," Annette beamed. "Incredible."

Charlene's decision hadn't just made Noah happy, apparently. Annette seemed moments away from bursting into happy tears.

"We're doing great," Charlene said. "How are you?"

"I'm better now." Elaine smiled, but this time, it didn't quite reach her eyes. "I'm trying to outwalk my problems."

Annette waved Elaine closer to the porch. "How about you talk them out instead?"

"No, no, no. No, I don't want to burden you girls with the problems of an old lady." Elaine wasn't more than ten or fifteen years older than Charlene, but sometimes she talked like she was old enough to be her mother twice over.

"I'm lighter than air right now," Annette said with a playful elbow to Charlene's side. "I could use a little burdening to bring me back to the ground. Lay it on us."

"If you want to," Charlene added.

Elaine moved to the end of the steps and rested an arm on the railing. "I promise I didn't come here to vent."

"I'm telling you, it's fine even if you did," Annette said.

"Thanks," Elaine sighed. "It would be nice to talk to someone about this. I've been thinking about this for a long time, but I'm still not sure what to do. I think I might have to move."

"What? Since when?" Charlene had been talking with Elaine for months about flipping and selling her own house, but Elaine had never said a thing about wanting to move.

"Since John died." Elaine shook her head. "I wanted to believe I could manage to stay in the house by myself. We had so many good memories there. I didn't want to lose John and our home at the same time. But I'm not sure I can afford it."

"Oh, Elaine. I'm so sorry. I know how that feels."

"I'm sorry, too," Annette added.

Elaine smiled at them both. "Thank you. It's a small thing in the grand scheme, but—"

"It's not small if it's big to you," Annette said.

Charlene nodded in agreement. "You could have told me this was going on. I'm always around if you need someone to talk to."

Yet another thing Charlene never would have said even a week earlier. But now she knew how nice it felt to have people to turn to. People to count on. She wanted to be that for Elaine.

"You girls are too sweet," Elaine said. "And Charlene, what about if I need someone to help me get my place on the market? Now that your house is done, maybe you could come flip mine? Do you mind getting paid in baked goods and fancy coffee drinks?"

Charlene laughed. "I wouldn't mind. But honestly, your house isn't a good candidate for a flip. It is beautiful just the way it is."

"And way too big," Elaine complained. "I've already talked to a realtor about listing it. He said the house would most likely be split into a duplex and used as vacation rentals. Maybe it makes me a snob, but I hate the thought of that."

"You're not a snob. That's your home. It makes sense you want it to stay intact."

"Plus, it would be a disservice to a beautiful home," Annette agreed.

"But I don't have much choice as far as I can see. Things can't carry on as they have been for too much longer. Something has to change."

"You know, I've come to learn recently that things have a funny way of working out," Charlene said. "I'm sure you'll figure out what to do, Elaine."

"Thanks, hon." Elaine winked. "Well, I won't keep you two."

"Keep us from what?" Annette asked, gesturing around the lawn. "We're parked here until the little guy tires of hunting. You've improved our night if anything."

"You're too sweet, but I forgot my bug spray. I'm getting eaten alive."

Charlene watched Elaine give Tyler a quick squeeze goodbye and move down the sidewalk, and she realized that maybe some of Tyler's optimism had already rubbed off on her. Because, for the first time in a long time, she truly did believe that things would work out. For herself and Elaine. And she hadn't felt that way in a long time.

It felt good.

Tyler smelled like dirt and bug spray. The moment they walked into the house, Charlene hustled him up the stairs to the bath.

She was severely lacking in bath toys—yet another thing to add to the never-ending list of things she needed to buy. She scrounged around in the kitchen for an old colander and a turkey baster for him to play with.

Fortunately, he was delighted with her selection. He plunged the turkey baster into the water and squeezed. A barrage of bubbles rose to the surface, and he grinned. "I want bubbles. Big bubbles!"

"I don't have any bubble bath," Charlene said. "I'll have to buy some."

Tyler frowned in thought. "Mommy had bubbles. She put them on her chin like hair."

"Mommy made a bubble beard?" Charlene liked the thought of Margaret playing with Tyler. Of course, it also made her heart throb like she'd been electrocuted.

"Like Santa." Tyler stuck out his belly and patted it. 'Ho! Ho! Ho!'"

It struck Charlene then that Tyler had a whole life before he'd come into hers. It seemed obvious now, but the thought genuinely hadn't occurred to her before. That he had memories and favorite activities and friends. That he might even miss his old life.

Since the moment she'd opened the door and found him on her porch, Charlene had thought this was her choice to make. But what if it wasn't solely hers? Tyler should have a say, too. Shouldn't he?

Charlene scooped up some of the bath water in a large plastic cup and poured it carefully over Tyler's head, careful not to get any in his eyes. "Hey, Tyler? Do you like it here?"

"At Grandma and Aunt Net's house?" he asked.

"Yeah. At Grandma and Aunt Net's house," Charlene said. "Do you like living here?"

Without thinking about it much, he offered up a gesture that was halfway between a nod and a shrug.

"Do you like your room?"

"My bed is big." He spread his arms out as far as they would go. "At home, I had a small bed. It was for babies."

"And you like the big bed?"

He nodded. "And the bath." He splashed his hands in the water. "Mommy only had a… a… a rain bath." He mimed rain drops falling over his head.

"A shower?"

"A shower," he repeated. "Mommy only had a shower. But I like baths."

"What about the bubble beard?" Charlene asked. "Where did you make bubble beards?"

"In the sink with the blue soap." Tyler plunged the colander underwater and brought it up, smiling as the water drained out in a deluge.

Charlene was scared to ask much more. She'd gone so long not knowing where Margaret was or how she was doing that the thought of knowing worried her. What if Margaret lived in squalor? What if her grandson had spent the last three years in filth and poverty, and Charlene had just been sitting at home entirely unaware?

The thought made her sick. It also made her want to see Margaret.

Charlene cleared her throat. "Well, if you want to, you can live here. With me."

"Forever?" Tyler looked up at her, his hazel eyes wide and innocent. He had no concept of what 'forever' meant. No idea what he was committing to.

"Yeah, forever." *Unless you run away, too.* Charlene pushed the thought away. "You could live with Grandma forever."

Tyler was quiet for a moment. Then he splashed both hands in the water, sending splatters up the tile walls. "Yay!"

Charlene's eyes swam with unshed tears. "You like that idea?"

He nodded. "I can keep my big bed?"

"It's all yours."

"Forever?" he asked again.

Charlene swallowed down the emotion rising in her throat and blinked away the tears in her eyes. She nodded. "Yes. Forever."

Tyler cheered again, and this time, Charlene didn't care that he was soaking wet and sending splashes everywhere. She leaned over the tub and pressed a kiss to his wet head.

12

TWO WEEKS LATER AT CHARLENE'S HOUSE

Annette came down the stairs in a yellow sundress, Tyler's little hand in hers. "Are you sure you don't want us to stay? Handsome Noah might like the company."

"Handsome Noah?" Tyler squished his face up in confusion.

Charlene groaned. "Now you definitely can't stay. He can't know you call him that."

"Why not? It's a compliment."

"It's unprofessional." Charlene stopped in front of a mirror in the hallway and adjusted her hair. "He's only coming over to deliver paperwork and go over more adoption classes I need to take."

"And one's hair must be perfect if you're going to be pouring over boring paperwork. Everyone knows that."

Charlene spun around and narrowed her eyes at her sister. "He's Tyler's caseworker. I want him to know I'm put together and responsible. That's it."

Annette rolled her eyes. "Sure, sure. Whatever you say."

There was no point in arguing with Annette. Charlene had learned that the hard way over the past two weeks. The day after the choking incident, Noah had come by to check on Charlene and bring her the leftovers from the fish he'd cooked. Charlene had been down at the beach with Tyler, but Annette had been home. Unfortunately.

"He packed you a doggy bag of food from your date," Annette had practically screamed the moment Charlene and Tyler stepped onto the property.

"What?"

Annette had responded by lifting the Tupperware high in the air and shaking it. "Handsome Noah brought you food from your date. He even cut it up into bite-size pieces for you. Probably so you won't choke when he isn't around."

"Not funny!"

"I wasn't trying to be funny." Annette shoved the container at Charlene when she stepped onto the porch. "He likes you, Char. A lot. I could tell."

"And you're the expert on this kind of thing?"

She'd nodded. "The top authority. And based on the way you're blushing, you like him, too."

"It's from the sun," Charlene had mumbled as she pushed through the front door to take the leftovers to the fridge.

She'd eaten them later that night, and they were delicious. On top of everything else, Noah was a wonderful cook. The fish was caramelized and lemony, the rice he paired it with was fluffy and seasoned with lemon pepper, and the simple roasted vegetables rounded out the entire dish. Charlene couldn't help but wonder what it all would have tasted like fresh... with Noah sitting right across the table from her.

Charlene bent down and pulled Tyler in for a quick hug. He was already dressed in his flamingo swim trunks and a short-sleeve water shirt. He'd become quite the beach bum since his arrival.

"You have fun and listen to Aunt Net, okay?" Charlene pressed a kiss to his forehead. "I'll meet you down at the beach when I'm done."

"Is Handsome Noah coming over?" he asked as he fiddled with the strings of his trunks.

Charlene shot a glare over his head at Annette. "*Mr.* Noah is coming over, but it won't be any fun. I wish I could go to the beach with you."

"No, she doesn't," Annette whispered. On their way out the door, Annette stuck her head through the crack. "If your 'meeting' runs long, be sure to hang a sock from the doorknob or something. Tyler is too young to see his grandma necking a man on the couch."

Charlene looked around for something to throw, but Annette laughed and closed the door before she could find anything.

It was just as well. Getting worked up over Annette's teasing only made her enjoy it more. It was always better to ignore Annette than let her think she was getting to you.

Because she wasn't getting to Charlene. Not at all. Charlene knew her own feelings. Besides, he was just a civil servant doing his job. His goal was to make sure Tyler had a safe, healthy environment to live and grow in. Once that was done, Charlene doubted she'd ever see him again.

When a knock sounded at the door a few minutes later, Charlene hurried across the entryway. Then she got self-conscious about how quickly she'd gotten to the door and decided to count to eight before she opened it.

When she finally did, Noah was standing on the porch wearing a pressed button-down, trousers, and a wide smile. "Good morning."

"Good morning. Come on in." Charlene stepped aside and tried not to take a deep breath as he passed. Smelling your caseworker was unprofessional.

"I ran into Annette and Tyler on my way in," he said.

Oh no. "Oh, yeah? They're headed down to the beach this morning."

"Cute kid." Noah walked straight to the table and started arranging his folder and papers on the surface. "I'm pretty sure he called me handsome."

Charlene's face flamed, but she tried to play it off. "Did he really? Kids say the darndest things, don't they? How funny!"

She thought she saw Noah look back over his shoulder at her with a raised brow, but Charlene couldn't be sure. She refused to make eye contact with him.

He dropped down into a dining room chair and, even though it was Charlene's house, gestured for her to join him. "I haven't seen you in a while."

Charlene sat across from him. Suddenly, her kitchen table seemed much too small. "Things have been busy around here. Annette and I have been trying to make Tyler's room a little more kid-friendly. Stuffed animals, a craft table, some educational books."

Noah chuckled. "If you're trying to convince me you're a good guardian for Tyler, you really don't need to. I'm on your side."

"No, I'm not—I wasn't— I just meant—" Charlene's shoulders sagged. "Okay, I was trying a little bit."

"Well, you're wasting your time," he said. "I'm already thoroughly impressed."

Warmth flooded Charlene's face. She spun away from the table to grab a plate of muffins from the counter. "Hungry? Annette and Tyler made muffins last night. Apple cinnamon and blueberry lemon."

"Blueberry lemon, please. I had two appointments early this morning, so I never ate breakfast." Noah plucked the muffin from Charlene's hand and took a big bite. "These are incredible."

"Aren't they? Annette is quite the baker."

"Do you bake at all?" he asked.

Charlene shook her head. "I wish. But I've never been much of a chef." Charlene hesitated. "But I do know how to cook a square meal, of course. Protein, grains, vegetables, dairy. Everything a growing boy—"

"Charlene." Noah looked up at her from under thick brows. "I'm not here to judge your worthiness as Tyler's caretaker. I'm just here to make sure the process is legal."

"I know. Right. I'm sorry." Charlene bit her lower lip. "I'm just a little nervous."

"Because of me? Why ever would you be nervous around me?" Noah may have been there on business, but his smile was all mischief.

Charlene rolled her eyes. "Anyway, what's the next legal step in the process, Caseworker Noah?"

Noah grinned and shook his head. Then they got to work. Charlene had already been taking courses online covering everything from childrearing methods to internet safety and cyberbullying. Noah introduced even more training Charlene would need.

"I know it's a lot, but we want you to be prepared for anything," he said.

Charlene waved him away. "It's okay. Tyler's worth it."

Noah smiled. "I'm glad to hear you say so."

He slid across another piece of paper. "And this is just a form that will indicate your official interest in adopting Tyler. It is for our bookkeeping in case another relative appears and has an interest in adoption, as well."

Charlene's eyes widened. "Is that possible?"

"Anything is possible," he said. "I've seen family members come out of the woodwork at the midnight hour time and time again. It can get ugly. I don't have any reason to assume that will be the case here, though. Do you?"

"I have no idea," Charlene said. "I'm not even sure who Tyler's father is. Margaret dated her drug dealer for a while, but beyond that... Even if he was the father, I wouldn't have the first clue as to how to contact either of them."

It was weird to think of Tyler having another set of grandparents. Charlene had already gotten used to being one of the few people in his life.

"That actually reminds me." Noah reached down and dug through a messenger bag until he pulled out a pad of paper with a pen clipped to the front cover. "I need to gather a little more family history from you."

"My family history?"

He nodded. "Margaret provided some information to the judge when she went to court to have her parental rights terminated, but the more we know about you and all the people around Tyler, the better we can facilitate this transition."

"Now I'm positive I'm talking to Caseworker Noah," Charlene mumbled. He sounded so professional.

"Sorry. I know this can be awkward," he winced. "But everything you say here is confidential, of course. And I suppose if you felt uncomfortable, I could have another caseworker assigned to Tyler's case and—"

"No!" Charlene reached across the table and grabbed Noah's hand. "It's fine. I'm not uncomfortable. Well, not with you, anyway." She laughed. "I'm just uncomfortable in general."

Noah chuckled. "Okay, that's good. I think?"

Noah's thumb twitched, and Charlene realized she was still holding onto his hand. She yanked her own back quickly and sat up nice and tall in her chair. "Where should I start?"

"The beginning."

Charlene wiggled her fingers in front of her face like she was setting a scene. "It was a hot summer night when my mother walked through the emergency room doors..."

Noah laughed. "Let me rephrase: the beginning of Tyler's story."

Charlene winked at him and then took a deep breath. "Well, I think that means starting with Davy's death. That's when things sort of fell apart for Tyler's mom."

"Your daughter Margaret, correct?" Noah asked. "I have to double-check all the details."

Charlene nodded. "My daughter, Margaret. Yes. She and her dad, Davy, were incredibly close. He connected with her in a way I was never able to. When he was diagnosed—"

"Cancer?" Noah asked quietly.

"Stage four glioblastoma," Charlene confirmed. "Brain cancer."

"I'm so sorry."

"Me too," Charlene said. "He made it twelve months, which is longer than the doctors predicted. But it wasn't long enough. It never would have been long enough. Not for me or Margaret."

"How old was Margaret?"

"Eighteen when he died. But just barely. Her birthday was the month before." Charlene took a deep breath. It had been a long time since she'd waded into that time of her life. Over the years, she'd found it was better not to dwell. "Davy wanted her to have a party with all of her friends, but he refused to come down out of his room. He didn't want to be a distraction. By that point, he was wheelchair-bound and hardly able to speak. He didn't want to embarrass her."

Noah winced and shook his head sadly. But he never looked away from Charlene, not even for a second.

"Margaret ended up cancelling the party day the of," Charlene continued. "Instead, she and her friends went out. She said ice skating, but now I'm not so sure."

"Why is that?" Noah asked.

"She came home late that night. She smelled like cigarettes and alcohol. I wasn't happy about it, but I cut her some slack. Assumed she and her friends were being typical teenagers. It wasn't until she ran away that I found the drugs. That's when I realized how bad things had gotten for her."

"You think it started after Davy's diagnosis?"

Charlene shrugged. "I think it got worse after Davy's diagnosis. How long it was happening before that? I have no idea. I guess… I guess I should have paid closer attention."

"Hey." Noah reached over and squeezed Charlene's fingers. "No parent can keep an eye on their kid all the time. They are people just like we are. Complex and secretive. You only get to know what they want you to know."

Charlene tried to give him a smile. "Maybe you're right."

"I am always right," he said confidently. "You can never know exactly what's going on in someone else's head. No matter how hard you try. Or how honest you think they're being."

Something dark flashed across Noah's face. An unusual sight for the usually chipper man. Charlene wanted to ask, but didn't want to pry.

"Is this your way of telling me you really are stalking me, but lied when I asked about it?"

He chuckled softly. "No, I was honest about that part."

Had he been dishonest about something else? Charlene almost didn't want to know. Maybe it would be best if they focused on Tyler and dropped all of the personal chatter.

"Did you know I was married?" Noah said suddenly. He set his pen down.

Charlene blanched. "N-no," she stammered. "I didn't know that."

Noah seemed like he was barely hearing her. "Yeah. For a while."

"Oh. Not... not anymore?"

He shook his head. "It fell apart, I guess you could say. But that phrase always sounds so sudden to me. It doesn't feel that fast while it's happening. I thought we wanted the same things. She *said* we wanted the same things. A big house, a happy family, a future together. And I took her words at face value. I proposed with my grandmother's engagement ring. I worked hard to save money and buy a big house. We started trying to have kids. But..." Noah pressed his lips together and sighed. "We couldn't seem to get pregnant."

Charlene could tell it was hard for him to find the words. "You don't have to tell me this, Noah. You don't owe me anything just because I have to tell you all of my problems."

He shook his head. "I'm not telling you because I owe you. I'm telling you because... because you're easy to talk to." He gave her a sad smile.

"And slightly because I want to make sure our relationship stays balanced."

Something tingled in Charlene's chest at the word "relationship." It could mean anything, really. No point in making a fuss about it.

"When we tried for a year with no luck, we went to a doctor and then a fertility clinic," he continued. "There were pills and vitamins and shots to take. It was a lot for her, but I thought it was what we both wanted. So I encouraged her. I tried to support her. I did my best to be there at every appointment and to help administer every shot. I wanted to help as much as I could."

"That's sweet," Charlene said.

Noah shrugged. "I thought so, too. But when we got the positive test—the long-awaited reward for all of the hard work and money and patience—I was ecstatic. And she was... not."

"Nervous?"

"Despondent, more like."

"Oh. She wasn't happy?"

Charlene remembered coming home from the doctor to tell Davy she was pregnant. She'd practically floated up the steps to the crummy little apartment they shared off-campus. "Happy" wasn't the right word. Charlene had been downright elated. Davy actually went out and bought the baby its first birthday cake from the grocery store. They'd eaten it straight from the plastic tin on their front porch.

"No, she wasn't happy," Noah confirmed. "She told me with tears in her eyes that I'd been suffocating her. That I'd been putting too much pressure on her to have a baby. So much so that she didn't recognize our relationship anymore. Not only was she not happy about the baby, but she wasn't happy with me at all."

"Oh my God, Noah. I'm so sorry."

"There had been warning signs, of course," he said. "But I didn't see them until later. Or I'd chalked them up to hormones because of the shots and pills. I assumed that once she was pregnant, we'd be happy again. But... I was wrong."

"I know how you feel," Charlene said. "Looking back, I can see the signs that something was wrong with Margaret. But it's easy to brush those worries aside when they're right in front of you. You want things to be fine, so you convince yourself they are."

"Exactly." Noah pushed out a big breath. "Anyway, long story short, she left me and met someone else before she even gave birth. Now my son sees his stepdad more than he sees me."

The story hit Charlene like a runaway train. She hadn't even realized Noah had a son, a family, a history. She hadn't thought to ask.

"He used to come down for the summers, but between baseball tournaments and sleepaway camps, he's busy these days."

"What's his name?"

Noah smiled. "Dean. He's a good kid. I'm glad he's happy and healthy and safe, all that. This just isn't how I imagined being a dad."

"If it makes you feel any better, this is not at all how I imagined being a mom," Charlene said. "Believe me, I get it."

Her hand was still laying on the table, and Noah reached over and brushed his fingers across hers. To her surprise, she didn't jerk away or pull back. She just watched Noah's hand make its slow ascent over the back of hers and towards her wrist.

When she finally looked up, Noah was watching her. His eyes shifted down to her lips. He was going to kiss her. It may have been a long time since Charlene had been kissed, but she knew the signs well enough.

This was happening. And she wasn't running away. In fact, Charlene was leaning towards Noah, as well. Her eyes fluttered closed and—

The solid wood front door slammed open. Charlene and Noah flew apart, breathless.

"We forgot sunscreen," Annette called into the house.

"And I have to potty!" Tyler said. A second later, Charlene could hear his footsteps padding up the stairs.

Annette appeared in the doorway a moment later, hands on her hips. "But mostly we came back for the sunscreen." She looked from Charlene to Noah with a casual smile. "Sorry to interrupt your boring paperwork."

Noah bit back a laugh. "You should be. I may never forgive you."

Charlene smiled and tried to hide her blush.

Maybe she should have followed Annette's advice and put a sock on the front door.

13

A FEW WEEKS LATER AT THE ISLE OF PALMS MARINA

It was a sweltering afternoon, the kind that would usually find Charlene hiding out in the air conditioning with iced tea and a book. But Tyler had seen some kids crabbing the day before, and now he wouldn't be satisfied until he tried it for himself.

"You're lucky you're cute, Ty." Annette mopped her brow with the hem of her tank top. "It's hot out here."

Tyler held onto the dip net with eager fingers. Tying the chicken necks to the line was more than he was willing to do, but he was ready to pounce the moment a crab tugged on the line. Which, of course, hadn't happened once in the hour they'd spent drowning in their own sweat at the end of the dock.

Charlene panted in agreement with her sister. "It's amazing what big hazel eyes can convince you to do, isn't it? I had other plans today, but here we are. Slowly melting."

Really, heat and humidity aside, Charlene was grateful for the distraction. Her only plans had involved texting her realtor for the umpteenth time about any possible leads on buyers for her house. After that, she needed to start the process of lining up some kind of daycare for Tyler. Elaine had watched him two different times so Charlene could go out to dinner with Noah—purely friendly occasions. And "Aunt Net" had been a huge help, but she had to get back to reality soon. School was starting up in a couple weeks and she couldn't live with Charlene forever.

"I should be apartment hunting," Annette sighed. "Never thought I'd hear myself say that again."

"I don't want to be a pest, but like I've said, there are schools around here."

"I know. But my job isn't why I ran away for the summer. I like my job."

Frederick sat like an elephant between the lines. Annette didn't like to talk about him. Since she'd explained the situation with his mistress the first night she'd arrived, his name hadn't come up once. It was as though he didn't exist.

"I'll just miss you." Charlene didn't want to say it, but she was afraid that if Annette left, she'd go another five years without seeing her.

Annette smiled at her over Tyler's head. "I'll come back to visit." Then she playfully pinched Tyler in the side until he giggled. "And this little guy has to come visit Aunt Net. Right, buster?"

"Right!" he squawked.

Hopefully, Annette's apartment would have a futon for visitors to crash on. Charlene had done her level best not to think about money over the last few weeks, but the mere thought of paying for a hotel on a trip to see her sister in Asheville was enough to make her gag.

"And who knows?" Annette continued. "Maybe a certain handsome DSS worker could join you for a trip."

Charlene rolled her eyes. "We are friends."

"I thought he was just Tyler's caseworker?"

"He can be both. Sue me. I have a friend. It is not a big deal."

"It's a big deal for you," Annette retorted. "You have a friend, number one. Number two, this friend is a man. Number three, this friend is a handsome, single man who clearly likes you and who you clearly like in return. Number four—"

"Okay, I get the point. You can stop counting."

Annette ignored her and kept going. "Number four, he is en route to meet us on one of the hottest days of the summer to go crabbing with a three-year-old. If that's not love, I don't know what is." She planted her hands on her hips in satisfaction. "Okay. Now, I'm done."

"Praise be to the heavens above," Charlene drawled.

Yes, she and Noah had been spending time together. But there hadn't been another near-kiss situation since the first one. In fact, Noah had been noticeably hands off. Probably because the one time he tried to hug her, she choked. And when he tried to kiss her, Annette and Tyler nearly caught them in the act. It was enough to dampen any person's spirits.

"When will he be here?"

Charlene checked her watch. "Half an hour. He took his boat out for some fishing this morning. He said he'll ride over here when he's done."

"Any plans for the afternoon?"

"He thought Tyler might enjoy a ride in the boat, so I thought he and I would go home with Noah. If that's okay with you?"

Annette waved a hand. "Of course. I wouldn't dare get in the way of that Hallmark moment waiting to happen."

Charlene decided to save her breath. Let Annette think what she wanted—Charlene knew the truth. There would be no high-tension romantic moments. Just a friendly boat ride.

For a few minutes, she lazed back in her folding chair. A slight breeze had picked up and cut through the oppressive heat nicely. Charlene closed her eyes and let herself doze.

Suddenly, a small body knocked into her leg and nearly sent her chair tumbling backwards. "The line moved! The line moved!" Tyler was jumping up and down like he'd just won the lottery.

"There's a tug," Annette confirmed. She grabbed the drop line and began pulling it in slowly. "Okay, Tyler. Give the net to Grandma. Let her grab the crab."

Tyler's hands tightened around the handle. "No! I wanna do it. I can do it!"

Annette shook her head. "Remember what I said? The crabs can pinch. You need to let Grandma grab it."

Charlene knelt down to Tyler's level. "I'll help you. Maybe we can both do it together."

"I wanna do it all by myself." Tyler's cheeks were turning red and his eyes were set in narrowed slits. He looked so very much like his mother at that age. Nothing good had ever come of it when Margaret got that fire in her eyes.

"I don't want him close to it," Annette argued. "He needs to stand back."

"Aunt Net," he growled, "I wanna do it!"

"Give it here. I'll just do it," Annette huffed. The crab was latched on the bait just below the surface of the water. They could see him swirling around in the murky green tide.

"I can help him," Charlene argued. "It will be fine."

"Do you remember when that crab pinched me?" Annette raised her brows in challenge. "I was sixteen and I cried for an hour. I'm not letting him near it."

The instance in question had been a dare. A Midwestern skater boy staying on the island for the summer had caught Annette's eye. He'd never seen a crab up close before, and Annette wanted to prove how brave she was. Instead, one crab pinch later, she'd cried until snot ran down her nose. The boy rode off on his skateboard and never spoke to her again.

"I'm right here with him. I can help," Charlene said.

"I wanna do it by myself!" Tyler swung the net in the air like a weapon.

Charlene jumped back to avoid getting hit and accidentally slammed into Annette. She yelped in surprise and stumbled backwards.

"Oh no!" Annette groaned. "We lost the crab."

Sure enough, the chicken neck was dangling a few inches above the water, crabless.

Tyler's frustration immediately mutated into devastation. His eyes went glassy and he tipped his head back and wailed. "I wanted to get it!"

Charlene patted his back. "I'm sorry, buddy."

"He should apologize," Annette grumbled.

Charlene shot her sister a warning look. "You should have let me help him with the net. It would have been fine."

"How is this my fault?"

"No one is saying it's your fault," Charlene sighed. "It is nobody's fault. It doesn't matter."

Annette dropped the line back in the water and crossed her arms. "Yes, it does. He doesn't listen." She bent down so she was on Tyler's level. "You didn't listen, and now we don't have any crab. We all sweated through our clothes for nothing."

"Annette! That's enough!" Charlene grabbed a bottle of Gatorade from the cooler and opened it for Tyler. "Here, buddy. Why don't you go see if you can spot any other crabs in the water?"

Tyler's lower lip was still sticking out in a pout, but he took the Gatorade and wandered off. His shoulders were sagged in defeat.

Charlene whirled on her sister. "What is wrong with you?"

"Me?" Annette's eyes flared. "I was trying to protect him. What is wrong with you? Do you want him to get hurt?"

"I was right there to help him. And besides, it was a tiny little blue crab, not a shark. He would have been fine."

"You don't know that!"

This was the heat talking. And hunger. And maybe, beneath all that, five years of buried feelings.

"You can't protect kids from everything," Charlene said.

"You can at least try!"

"If you do, then they never get to experience anything for themselves. He would have been fine. It was his idea to go crabbing. You should have at least let him try."

Annette stepped back. "Thanks for the parenting advice, Char. You're clearly the expert, right?"

The words cracked through the air like a whip. Charlene winced back. "What is that supposed to mean?"

"I spend nine months out of the year educating kids, and you don't even know where yours lives. But what do I know about children, right? I've never had one of my own, so I'm useless."

Angry tears burned the backs of Charlene's eyes, but she blinked them away. "That isn't what I said."

"It's what you meant, though." Annette wrapped the line loosely around a metal hook sticking out of a post. "You gave birth, so I don't have a say. You're better at this than me, so I should just leave it all to you. Did I miss anything in there?"

"I'm the one who is going to adopt him," Charlene said. "So, yeah—you should leave the discipline to me. That's my job."

Annette let out a humorless laugh. "And here I thought we were in this together. But I guess I'll always be second fiddle to you, huh?"

"What does that even mean?"

"Nothing!" Annette threw up her hands and backed away. "It doesn't mean anything. But it's clear I'm not much of an asset here. I think I'm just going to go home."

"Annette, come on," Charlene pleaded. "You don't have to—"

"I'll see you at home." And with that, Annette turned and marched off down the pier.

Charlene watched her go, bubbling up inside with feelings that she didn't quite know how to name.

A few seconds later, Tyler appeared at Charlene's leg. "Where's Aunt Net?"

"She's going home." Charlene smoothed her fingers through his sandy brown hair. "We'll see her later. Do you want to catch another crab?"

In typical kid fashion, Tyler immediately forgot everything that had happened in the last ten minutes. His emotional slate was wiped clean. Once again, he was just pure excitement as he flopped back on his belly to stare into the depths of the waves lapping at the dock pillars.

Charlene wished she had that kind of resilience. The ability to forget the past. To start fresh.

God knows she needed it.

When Noah strolled down the dock ten minutes later, Charlene and Tyler had just caught their first and only crab of the day.

"Mr. Noah! Look!" Tyler jumped up and down next to the cooler where the day's catch was being kept. "I got a crab! I got a crab all by myself."

Noah grinned. "Is that right? You didn't have any help?"

"Grandma pulled in the line, but he scooped it out of the water all on his own," Charlene confirmed.

Noah held out his hand for a high-five. "Atta boy! You're a natural born crabber, Tyler."

The brown paper lunch sack Noah was carrying with him didn't last long. Tyler snatched it out of his hand the moment he learned there was food inside. In a matter of minutes, they were all digging into bologna and cheese sandwiches still cold from Noah's ice chest.

"Where's Annette?" Noah asked, holding up a fourth sandwich. "I thought she was coming, too."

"She did, but she, uh… left."

Noah's brows pinched together, but Charlene just shook her head. She didn't want to get into it right now. "Did you catch anything this morning?" she asked instead.

"Enough," Noah shrugged. "My deep freeze will be well-stocked for the next couple weeks, at least. You'll have to come over and help me eat it."

Charlene's face flushed. "Are you sure that's a good idea?"

"Absolutely. I'll be sure to brush up on my CPR skills, just in case." Noah's eyes twinkled with mischief.

Charlene elbowed him in the side. "You're really not funny."

"Who said I was joking?"

Charlene gasped, but couldn't keep the smile off her face. "Really, *really* not funny."

Apparently, it had been long enough that they could joke about her near-choking incident. At the time, Charlene had thought she'd never recover. But now, even she had to admit it was funny.

"I'm serious, though," Noah said. "Not about the CPR, but about you coming over for dinner. When are you free?"

An hour earlier, Charlene would have said anytime. *Tonight. Right now.* But now…

"I'll have to check with Annette," she said. "See if she's up for babysitting. She might need a bit of a break."

"Oh?"

"Yeah. We had a long day of crabbing."

Charlene wanted to chalk the entire fight up to the heat and hunger. She didn't want to think that things between her and her sister could be fracturing already. Not after the last month. Not after things had been going so well.

So, for now, she wouldn't dwell. It was time to practice being a little more like Tyler. To let the emotions of the past slip away. To focus on the positives. Where to start? She finally had lunch in her system. Tyler had caught a crab. And Noah was here. What else could Charlene really ask for in that moment?

Tyler crumpled up the Saran wrap from his sandwich and stood up on his tiptoes. His eyes scanned the water. "Where's the boat?"

Noah waved a hand towards the set of docks around the corner. "I parked at a dock a-ways away. You can't see it from here."

"Do I still get to go in the boat?" It was the most serious Charlene had ever seen the three-year-old's face. She had to bite back a laugh.

"Of course!" Noah said. "A promise is a promise, isn't it? I'm a man of my word."

Tyler literally jumped for joy. "Can we go right now?"

"Are you done crabbing?" Charlene asked. "If you want to stay here and try to catch another crab, then—"

"I want the boat!" Tyler said. "No more crabs."

Noah laughed. "Well, if your grandma agrees, then I don't see why we can't—"

Before he could even finish, Tyler launched himself at Charlene's leg. "Please, Grandma? Can we go? I wanna ride the boat."

Charlene ruffled his hair. "Of course, buddy. Let's pack up our stuff and we can head that way."

Tyler ran around picking up trash and running it to the trash can a little further down the pier while Charlene and Noah gathered up the crabbing supplies. There weren't many, so it didn't take long before they were walking together down the pier. To be fair, Noah and Charlene did most of the walking. Tyler kept running ahead and then pogoing in place impatiently while he waited for the old folks to catch up.

"I'd kill for that much energy," Noah chuckled.

"Right?" Charlene laughed. "You see the way he's jumping around right now? Imagine that at the end of your bed at five in the morning."

"Five in the morning?" Noah whistled. "That's early."

"And it feels even earlier when you're being sloshed around by a hyper three-year-old."

Noah laughed. "But you kind of love it, right?"

"Kind of," Charlene admitted. "It brings back good memories. When Margaret was his age, Davy and I would wake up to noises coming from her bedroom. We'd go in to check and find her dressed up in her fanciest outfits, having pretend tea with her stuffed animals. At two and three in the morning, mind you!"

"That's adorable. My ex told me Dean had night terrors. I never witnessed one, but… I'm sure a stuffed animal tea party is better than that."

"Absolutely."

Charlene took Noah's offered hand as he helped her down the wooden stairs. It was completely friendly. A comforting gesture, if anything. And the butterflies in her stomach were just a coincidence.

When they got to the boat, Noah strapped Tyler into a kid's life vest and they loaded up. Tyler darted from one side of the boat to the other, leaning over the side and staring at his reflection in the water. When the engine started up, he squealed in delight. And when they actually started driving? Well, Charlene didn't think she'd ever seen a purer form of joy.

Tyler's hair whipped in the air and his eyes squinted against the spray of the water with every bounce of the vessel. When Noah zigzagged through the water, Tyler tried to balance in the middle. He held both arms out and giggled as he stumbled around.

Noah turned and caught Charlene's eye in all the madness. He winked —just once, so simple and subtle and easy that it took her breath away. Charlene couldn't imagine anywhere else she'd rather be.

14

AFTERNOON AT CHARLENE'S HOUSE

The driveway was empty when Noah dropped Charlene and Tyler off at her house. "Annette still not home?" There was concern in Noah's voice.

It had been easy for Charlene to forget about her problems when they'd been zipping across the water in Noah's boat. When Tyler had been clinging to Charlene for stability and giggling every time the boat sprayed a fine mist of saltwater in their faces.

But on the drive home, Tyler had fallen asleep. That was all well and good, but the quiet had given Charlene far too much time to dwell. Her fears were probably tattooed all over her face.

"I'm sure she just went to run an errand. Nothing's wrong." Charlene whispered so she wouldn't wake Tyler, but also because she was sure that if she said it loudly enough, it'd be obvious that it was a lie.

Charlene lifted Tyler out of his car seat and smiled warmly at Noah in a silent thanks for the fun afternoon.

"You sure you don't want me to carry him up?" Noah asked.

Charlene waved him away. "I can do it. But thanks."

"Alrighty then. Y'all have a good night."

"You, too, Noah."

Tyler stirred once as Charlene nestled him into his bed, but he was beyond exhausted and fell immediately back to sleep. She turned out his light and backed out of the room.

As she walked down the stairs, the front door opened. Annette was home.

She looked up at Charlene and then quickly away. The tension between them was thick, but Charlene was anxious to cut through it. To make things okay again.

"Tyler's asleep," Charlene said. "He was exhausted."

"That makes two of us." Annette toed off her sand-covered sandals at the door. "I bought a sandwich and went for a walk along the beach."

"I thought bike rides were the best way to clear your head?"

"Not according to you," Annette smirked. "Although maybe I should have given it a try. See if a handsome man would stop and help me massage out my leg cramp."

Charlene chuckled. "Noah didn't massage me."

They fell into a thick silence again. Charlene could tell Annette was trying. Neither of them *wanted* to be in a fight.

"Hey," Charlene said softly, "I'm sorry about what happened at—"

"No, I'm sorry." Annette shook her head. "I was hot and hungry."

"That's what I figured."

"And jealous." Annette rolled her lips nervously. "I'm sorry."

Charlene frowned. "Jealous? Of what?"

Annette gestured vaguely. "Of you. *This.* Tyler." She sighed. "You're figuring things out, you know? Between Tyler and Noah…"

"I'm sorry—what?" Charlene huffed out a laugh. "You think I'm figuring things out?"

"You've always had your life together."

Charlene couldn't believe what she was hearing. She felt like she needed to sit down. "How on earth do you figure *that*?"

"Come on, Char. You know what I mean." Annette raised a brow. "You knew that you wanted to study architecture when you were fifteen years old. You got early acceptance to Clemson."

"And dropped out because I got pregnant," Charlene argued.

"Because you fell in love and got married," Annette retorted. "Most people would call that a win."

"I wouldn't. I mean, I loved Davy. And I chose to have Margaret. I was excited, but..." Charlene shrugged. "I had to give up my degree to raise her. That wasn't my plan."

"Yeah, but you pivoted. You always seem to have a plan. To know which move to make next. I've never had that."

Charlene didn't know whether she should laugh or cry. "Are you kidding? I had no idea how to handle Davy's death. Or Margaret running away. I didn't have a plan. I never have."

"But you held things together. You kept flipping houses and—"

"I buried myself in work," Charlene corrected. "I kept doing what I'd always done because... well, I just didn't know what else to do. I lost everyone. My husband, my daughter... My sister."

Annette looked down at her bare feet. "I'm sorry."

"Can I ask you something?" The question Charlene had wanted to ask for over five years was finally coming out. And she didn't know if she was ready for the answer. "Why did you leave?"

Annette shook her head. "You'll hate me when you hear the truth."

"No, I won't."

"Don't be so sure." Annette chewed on her bottom lip. "I left because… because I'd been waiting a long time for your life to fall apart."

Charlene blinked. "What?"

"It makes me sound horrible." Annette ran a hand down her face. "But I'd been waiting to be the sister who had it all together—the great job, the loving husband, the adorable family. And then your life did fall apart. And I still felt terrible." She grimaced like it was hurting her to say these things out loud. "It's not like I wanted Davy to die, of course. But… I just thought seeing you struggle would make me feel better about myself. And instead, I felt like a monster. It was hard to be around you without feeling guilty."

Charlene didn't know what to say. Never once in the forty years she'd known her sister had she ever thought Annette felt this way. She didn't know how to process it.

"Now, I know your life wasn't perfect. But I thought it was back then," she said. "And I just couldn't stand comparing myself to you all the time."

"But you and Frederick were always whisking off on amazing vacations and—"

"Doing anything to avoid sitting together in our house with nothing to distract us," Annette interrupted. "Frederick and I weren't best friends the way you and Davy were. And I hated that we kept trying and trying to have kids, and it wouldn't happen."

Charlene held up a hand to stop her. "I thought you didn't want kids."

"I convinced myself and everyone else that was true for a while. But I wanted them so bad. I still do." She snorted. "And now Frederick is having one with his mistress. Go figure. Whereas I'm alone, looking for an apartment while I come to terms with the fact that parenthood will probably never happen for me. Not now. Meanwhile, you are getting a second chance with—"

"Tyler isn't a do-over."

"I know that. I'm sorry. I didn't mean for it to sound like—"

"It's okay," Charlene said. "It really is. But I just need you to know that there is nothing I can do to fix the mistakes I made with Margaret. No matter how hard I try to move forward or make amends, the fact is that my only child fell through the cracks. And it's all my fault."

"Charlene, that isn't true."

"It is," Charlene said. "And honestly, taking Tyler is selfish on my part. I'm not the best choice for him. I know that. But on some level… well, maybe you were onto something when you told me Tyler isn't a flip house."

Annette shook her head. "I didn't mean that. I was upset."

"But you made a good point. He isn't a project I can take on and fix up. He's a little boy. A whole human. And he needs to be loved and taken care of for who he is. Not because I need to make myself feel better or try to rewrite the past."

The more she spoke out loud, the less certain she felt. Charlene had thought her motivations were pure, but maybe they'd been warped all along. Maybe she was going through the adoption proceedings for the wrong reasons. Trying to prove to herself and everyone else that she could be a good parent after all.

"Charlene…" Annette finally pushed away from the door and moved to the base of the steps. "All of this baggage is mine, okay? You're doing great. Don't let my problems make you doubt yourself."

Too late. The seed had been planted. Charlene could feel it taking root.

She waved a dismissive hand. "It doesn't matter. The important thing is that you and me are okay now. Are we okay?"

Annette hesitated for a moment, studying Charlene. Then she smiled. "We're okay. Of course we're okay."

"No more secrets?"

"No more secrets," Annette agreed.

"You won't disappear again?"

Annette made a cross over her heart. "Promise. You're stuck with me."

Charlene pulled her sister into a tight hug. That was music to her ears. Because as much as Annette seemed to think Charlene's life was falling into place, Charlene felt like she might need someone to depend on in the days ahead.

She didn't have her happily ever after just yet.

For whatever time was left in Tyler's nap, Charlene wanted to sleep, too. She hadn't been kidding about the five AM wake up calls that more closely resembled a WWE wrestling match. Charlene had always been an early riser, but being body-slammed by a toddler before the sun was up was pushing it even for her.

Before she laid down, though, she reached for her phone. She'd left it behind on the charger after forgetting to charge it the night before. Somewhat surprisingly, there was a missed call.

The number was unknown, but they left a message.

"Hello, Charlene! This is Felicia from Safe Harbor Adoption Agency. I've been trying to make contact with you for the last few weeks, but haven't heard back. I understand this can be an overwhelming process, and I don't want to add to that. However, I did want to let you know that if you are still interested in seeking adoption, we do have a family who we think could be a

good fit for Tyler. I won't bother you again, but I wanted to relay the information so you can make a fully informed decision. I hope all is well."

Charlene listened to the message twice. There was a family out there. A family who wanted Tyler. Two parents, a home. Maybe they even had other children. Or a dog. Tyler would love having a dog. Whoever it was, they'd probably already been thoroughly vetted by the agency. No skeletons lurking in their closets. No red flags.

Her thought spiral was interrupted by her phone ringing. Immediately, Charlene assumed it was Felicia calling back. The urge to throw her phone was overwhelming. But when she looked down, a familiar named flashed on the screen.

Charlene picked up. "Hey, Jamie."

"Charlene," Jamie sing-songed. "I am your fairy god-realtor today because I am about to make all your dreams come true."

Charlene sat up in bed. "You have a buyer?"

"Do I ever! I've been telling everyone I talk to about your house and the property and all the work you've done. And it looks like my legwork has paid off. You have an offer, sight unseen."

"No way!" Charlene grinned. "Someone is interested?"

"More than interested," she said. "I was talking to my contractor friend, Larry, and I told him about your house. Well, his brother is looking to move and wants a big place close to the water with a lot of charm and character."

"That's my house!" Charlene said.

"Which is exactly why I sent Larry the listing pictures to show to his brother," she said. "Within ten minutes of sending the picture, I had a message in my inbox that will blow your socks off."

"Hurry and blow them off please." Charlene was practically bouncing up and down on the bed. Tyler was rubbing off on her.

"He is willing to give you an all-cash offer for the full listing price!"

Charlene squealed. "You're kidding! That could mean closing in, what, like two weeks?"

"Especially since he is waiving the inspection," she said. "Larry told his brother I'm trustworthy, so he's ready to sign as soon as you are."

This was it. Exactly what Charlene had been hoping for, falling right in her lap. She could sell her house, pay off her debts, and start over. Charlene could see it all so clearly—a bright future stretching out in front of her. Something she hadn't imagined for herself in a long time. No debt, no responsibilities, no—

Then she saw Tyler in her mind's eye. His chubby cheeks, his bright hazel eyes.

What did this mean for him?

She loved him. She knew that. But was that a good enough reason to deprive him of a future of his own? One where he could have a whole family surrounding him with love. One without all the baggage and heartbreak Charlene brought to the table.

Charlene was being offered her fresh start. But what about Tyler's?

"Okay." Jamie transitioned into her professional voice. "I am prepared to tell the buyer whatever you want. But I mean, you're taking this deal, right? Full price, cash offer, no inspection. It doesn't get better than that."

"It really doesn't," Charlene agreed. So why was her stomach in knots?

There was a soft knock on her bedroom door, and then Annette poked her head in. "Hey, Noah is here to see you." Charlene frowned and arched a questioning eyebrow, but Annette just shrugged. "He didn't say what he needed. Just that he wanted to see you."

Charlene mouthed a silent thanks and then squeezed her eyes closed. "Hey, Jamie? I'm going to have to call you back. I have... something came up."

"Okay, not a problem. But let me know soon. He's eager to buy, and I don't think he'd hesitate to jump on another house should it come up."

The knot in Charlene's stomach tightened. "Okay, will do. Thanks again."

The elation from a few minutes earlier was swirling in a big, mixed-up pot of emotions now. Charlene had no idea what to do. About anything.

Noah was standing on the front porch with his back to her. As soon as the door opened, he spun around and grinned. "Hey. Tyler forgot his turtle hat in the truck. I thought he might miss it."

"He would. It's his favorite. Thanks." Charlene had bought the hat for him the week earlier. It was a cheap souvenir hat with a cartoon turtle embroidered on the front. It would probably fall apart before he outgrew it. But Tyler already refused to leave home without it.

"More importantly," Noah murmured, "I was already missing you."

Charlene heard him, but distantly. Her mind was a thousand miles away. When she reached for the hat, Noah didn't let go. Instead, he tilted his head to the side and gave her an odd look. "What's going on?"

"Nothing," she said innocently. "Tyler is napping. I was actually going to lay down, too. I'm exhausted."

Noah shook his head. "This is more than that. Something is wrong. What is it?"

Sometimes it was frustrating how easily Noah seemed to be able to read her. "We don't need to get into it. It's not a big deal."

He pointed to her forehead, which she hadn't realized until that second was creased in worry. "If it's making your forehead like that, it is a big deal."

Charlene sighed. "I just got a couple phone calls and… it's not a big deal."

Noah raised a brow. "Don't make me ask again."

He was being playful, trying to draw her out. But there was a serious undertone. He wanted to be a person Charlene could talk to. A person she trusted. And Charlene wanted that, too. More than anything.

She walked to the wicker bench in front of the large picture window and dropped down in a heap. "I got an offer on my house."

"That's great!" Noah sat down next to her and draped his arm over the back of the bench. His fingertips brushed her shoulder. "Isn't it? I thought that's what you wanted."

"It was—It is." Charlene sighed. "It's great. Exactly what I've been hoping for. But I'm not sure what it means."

"It means someone wants to buy your house. What do you mean you don't know what it means?" Noah chuckled. "Try saying that five times fast."

"Originally, my plan had been to sell the house and start over. As much as I will always love Davy, I don't want to be reminded of him all the time. Of him or Margaret. I need a fresh slate."

"Sure, that makes sense," Noah said. "That makes perfect sense, actually. I sold my house after the divorce. It's hard to live in a place with so many memories."

"Exactly," Charlene said. "The offer is great, and a few weeks ago I would have jumped on it without any hesitation. But now…"

Noah nodded slowly in understanding. "Oh. Tyler."

"Tyler," Charlene repeated. "Exactly. I can't help but wonder if I'm... if I'm doing the right thing by him."

Noah's arm slid off the back of the bench and wrapped around Charlene's shoulders. "That's a perfectly normal thing to question. Every parent or guardian has these doubts. But Tyler will be happy no matter where you live. He doesn't care about the location. He cares about you."

Charlene felt like she could be sick. "But what if that isn't enough?"

"What do you mean?"

"I mean..." Charlene took a deep breath and tried to find the right words. "What if I'm making a mistake? With him... *for* him. I tried the parenting thing once and it didn't go well. And I had help back then. Davy was so much better with kids. And with teens. And with people, in general. It has never been my strong suit."

Noah leaned away from her to get a better look at her face. "Where is this coming from?"

"From me," Charlene said. "I just don't know if I'm the right person to take care of Tyler."

He pulled his arm back and folded his hands in front of him. "And who do you think would be the right person?"

Charlene shrugged. "That's the other part. I just got a call from Felicia, the woman from Safe Harbor. Apparently, they have a family they think could be a good fit and—"

"Adoption?" Noah pushed himself off the bench and paced across the porch. "You're back to wanting to send him away?"

"I'm not *sending him away*," she argued. "I'm trying to think about what's best for him and—"

"You're thinking about what's best for you," he snapped.

His sudden anger surprised her. After all, this was his line of work. He'd suggested Charlene go to Safe Harbor in the first place.

"I don't understand where this is coming from," she said. "I thought it was important that this arrangement worked for me, too. Isn't that what you said? What's so wrong with making sure this is what I want?"

Noah planted his hands on his hips and stared at her. "Nothing. Nothing is wrong with that. Because if your own comfort is your main concern right now, then maybe you aren't the best person to take care of Tyler, after all."

"Hey! That's not—"

"If you say 'fair,' I'll lose my mind." Noah pinched the bridge of his nose like he had a sudden migraine. "Do you have any idea how many situations I walk into every single day where things aren't *fair*? Children living in abusive situations. Children going hungry because their parents spent the last of the welfare money on drugs. Then I watch as these kids tumble their way through the system. Some get adopted, some bounce around from foster home to foster home until they turn eighteen and then get busy restarting the cycle with kids of their own. Or they end up without a family on the street. Does any of that seem *fair*?"

Whatever Charlene had wanted to say was now lodged in her throat. She couldn't swallow it down.

"And then here's Tyler," Noah continued. "This sweet kid who has a family member who can take care of him. A grandma who is stable and loving and kind. And you're taking that away from him. For what?"

Charlene had never seen Noah this way. He was angry. Truly angry. At her.

"I don't see it as taking anything away from him," Charlene said softly. "I think it could be giving him something. A chance at a better future."

Noah squeezed his eyes closed and then backed away. "I can't do this anymore."

"Noah, please," she said.

"No, no." He shook his head. "I should have known better than to get emotionally involved in a case. It was dumb of me. I just thought... I thought you were different."

Tears burned her eyes, but Charlene didn't know what to say.

With Noah, she felt like a better person. He looked at her in a way that made her feel whole and safe and loved. But now, the way he was looking at her... she'd never felt so low.

"I'm going to have another caseworker assigned to your case," he said. "If there even still is a case. You can't seem to make up your mind one way or the other. Maybe you can call Felicia back and work with her. I don't know. But I'm done."

"Noah!" Her voice broke around his name. "Just let me explain. I'm not happy about this either, but—"

He waved his hands in the air to cut her off and walked down the steps. Charlene stood marooned on the porch as he climbed up into his truck and drove away.

When Charlene turned around, Tyler's turtle hat was sitting on the bench where Noah had been only a moment before. And that silly hat, of all the things in her world, is what pushed her over the edge.

Charlene dropped down onto the bench and cried.

15

NEXT MORNING AT THE BEACH

"Where are their mommies?"

Charlene snapped her attention to where Tyler was crouched in the sand. Daily beach walks had taught him to stay safely behind the caution tape that wound around the turtle's nest. Occasionally, he got too excited and Charlene had to remind him of the rules. But she could hardly blame him. Just like Charlene, he couldn't wait to see them hatch.

"In the ocean," Charlene explained. "The moms lay their eggs in the sand and then go back to the water."

"Will the babies find their mommies after they hatch?"

Charlene sat down in the sand and tucked her legs underneath her. "No. The ocean is too big of a place. And their mommies are really far away."

He frowned. "They are all alone?"

This conversation felt too laced with meaning. Charlene hadn't gotten nearly enough sleep for this. After Noah had stormed off, she'd fumbled her way through an afternoon of building blocks in the living room and coloring at the dining room table. The moment Tyler was in his room for the night, Charlene went to bed herself.

But she didn't sleep. She tossed and turned restlessly. A few times, she managed to slip into a dream, but Noah starred in all of them. She'd be so happy to see him until he looked at her, oozing disappointment. It made Charlene feel two inches tall. She'd startle awake and begin the sleepless cycle all over again.

"What about their daddies?" Tyler continued. "Or their grandma? Do they have a grandma?"

Tears welled in Charlene's eyes and she turned away from Tyler so he wouldn't see. "I think it's about time you started school."

"School?" he asked.

"Yeah. So you can get answers to all the questions you have." She playfully pinched his cheek. "You could have a teacher who would be able to tell you anything you wanted to know. And classmates. Friends you could play and learn with. Does that sound fun?"

He sat up on his knees and grinned. "Yeah! I want to go to school."

"Have you ever been to school before?" *Before you came to live with me. Before your mom abandoned you on my front porch.* She hated that delineation in his life. Before and after. And she hated that she was thinking about making yet another: before and after staying with Grandma.

His forehead creased in thought. "No. Miss Kelly's wasn't school."

"No, Miss Kelly was daycare."

"Daycare," he agreed. "Not school. I've never been to school."

"Maybe you can go to one soon," she murmured. It seemed like a good idea to her. Of course, the decision would be left to whoever became his legal guardian.

That wouldn't be her.

Charlene pushed aside the guilt that welled up in her and tried to focus on the morning. To let her worries and emotions ebb away with the tide.

After they thoroughly investigated the turtle nest and the surrounding sand for any signs of hatchlings, Charlene and Tyler walked down to the surf and dipped their toes in the water. Tyler ran and sloshed around until the bottom few inches of his shorts were soaked. Only once he was good and sandy was he ready to walk back up to the house.

"I want to help Aunt Net bake cookies," Tyler said. "Chocolate cookies. With marshmallows."

"Oh, that would be such a good idea, but Aunt Net isn't home right now. Maybe later, hon."

Annette still had a couple more weeks before she needed to be back at work, but there was a lot of prep work still to do. She'd gone into Charleston earlier that morning to hunt down deals on craft paper and bulletin board decorations at a teacher supply store.

Charlene still worried her sister's return to Asheville would mark the end of their summer reconciliation, but she tried to shove down that bad feeling along with the rest. Between the adoption agency's voicemail and the all-cash buyer waiting for Charlene's approval, she had enough on her plate as it was. No need to add to it.

"She's home!" Tyler suddenly shouted. He jumped up and down and pointed to the porch. "I see her!"

Charlene followed Tyler's pointed finger. They were just coming over the dune that ran in front of her house. The deep porch was shaded, but Charlene could see someone standing just to the right of the steps.

But she knew it wasn't Annette.

The person was too thin. Even from across the lawn, Charlene could see pointed elbows and one skeletal knee sticking out from behind the banister.

"I don't think that's Aunt Net." Charlene grabbed Tyler's hand more tightly to keep him from running ahead of her. "I don't know who—"

Then the figure stepped out of the shadows.

And Charlene's heart slammed to a stop.

As the years had passed, Charlene had released the hope that she'd one day see her daughter again. It hurt too much to be continually disappointed time and time again. But now, here she was. Standing in front of her in the flesh.

Margaret.

Charlene couldn't breathe.

Margaret walked down the stairs and knelt down on the front walk, arms open. "Hi, baby! Mommy missed you!"

Charlene could feel Tyler stiffen. His hand went rigid in hers. She massaged her thumb over his little knuckles. "Honey, why don't you go inside and get one of the squeeze yogurts from the fridge drawer?"

The snacks were his favorite, and Charlene had teased that she might need to get a lock on the refrigerator to keep him from eating the entire box.

"All by myself?" He looked up at Charlene and blinked.

Sometime in the last few weeks, Charlene had stopped looking at Tyler and seeing Margaret in his face. The green and gold-flecked hazel eyes had become entirely his own. Now, when Charlene looked at him, she saw Tyler. Just Tyler.

Thank God for small mercies.

She ruffled his hair. "All by yourself. I'll be inside in a minute."

Tyler hesitated in front of his mom for a second before he skirted a wide path around her and disappeared inside the house.

"What have you been telling him about me?" Margaret stood up and brushed herself off.

Margaret wouldn't make eye contact with Charlene, which gave Charlene plenty of time to assess her appearance. To notice the sickly bruises on her arms and legs, the visible veins. The dusky blonde hair she'd always shared with Davy hung limp and lifeless over her face.

And her face. *Oh, goodness, her face.* Margaret didn't look twenty-three. She looked thirty-five, forty, a million.

For the last five and a half years, Charlene had imagined Margaret the way she'd looked the day she'd left home. Young and vivacious and healthy. Looking at her now felt like rewatching a favorite movie from your childhood and realizing it wasn't what you remembered. The way the reality could never quite match the memory in your head.

Five years of unspoken questions sat on her tongue. *Hello, how have you been? Where have you been? Are you okay?* But Charlene couldn't force them out.

"I haven't told him anything," Charlene said instead.

Margaret snorted. "Sure."

"I haven't," she insisted. "Your actions spoke loudly enough."

Finally, Margaret looked up. Charlene had to bite back a wince. The darkness under her daughter's eyes wasn't from smudged eye makeup the way it used to be. They were deep, dark circles pressed under her eyes by hard life experience.

"It has only been a few weeks. It's not like I abandoned him on the side of the road," she said.

"No, you just abandoned him on my doorstep." How many times had Charlene played this conversation out in her head? She'd dreamed up lectures she'd give to Margaret. Pleas she'd make to get Margaret to stay, to get help. But now, she couldn't move beyond the simplest explanations. "You abandoned your own son."

"Oh, and you're one to talk?" Margaret raised a thin brow. The accusation was plain enough.

"You ran away, Margaret. There's a difference."

"And you really went out of your way looking for me," she fired back. "Some concerned mother you were."

"I did look. Of course I looked. But what did it matter? Even if I'd found you, you wouldn't have come back."

"Why would I come back to live with the person who killed my dad?" The vicious words were spoken casually, but Charlene knew darn well that Margaret was wielding them like a weapon. Her aim was to hurt.

Charlene swallowed back a lump in her throat. "You don't really believe that."

Margaret crossed her arms over her chest. The tank top she wore was loose with a low-scooped neck. Charlene could see her ribs protruding through her skin. "I know what happened."

"No, you don't," Charlene said. "Your dad wanted to stop treatments. He was tired of fighting. He wanted to be at peace."

"He swore to me he'd never stop fighting," Margaret snapped. "He told me he'd fight as long as he could."

"And he did. He fought as long as he could. He fought until he couldn't fight anymore."

"He only gave up because you convinced him to!"

Charlene squeezed her eyes closed and took a deep breath. In her mind's eye, she could see Davy laying in the hospital bed that had been rolled into the guest room for him. He'd been frail and thin—much like Margaret was now, though for vastly different reasons.

He'd grabbed Charlene's hand and pulled her close. "It's time for me to go," he'd mumbled. "I'm ready."

Charlene had held it together for Davy, but that night when she was alone in their bedroom, she'd broken down and cried. Some part of her had believed there'd be a miracle. She'd expected Davy to be the one person who could fight the odds and overcome. But he couldn't and he hadn't and as much as Charlene hated the thought of life without him, it had been the right time to let him go.

"I never convinced your dad of anything," Charlene said softly. "It was always his choice. He had to sign the Do Not Resuscitate papers. He had to finalize his will. He helped plan his own funeral, for God's sake. He was ready to stop fighting."

Margaret stared daggers at her mother. "Only because his own wife wasn't fighting for him. Just like you didn't fight for me. You only care about yourself."

Her argument with Noah the day before crystallized in her mind. She could once again see the disappointment in his eyes after she told him she might not want to adopt Tyler. *I thought you were different...*

Charlene had tried to do the right thing by Davy, and he'd died. She'd tried to do the right thing by Margaret, and she'd run away. And now she was trying to do the right thing by Tyler, but no one seemed to believe her. Once again, Charlene was tearing herself apart to help someone and not a soul alive seemed to notice or care.

"What do you think I'm doing right now?" Charlene asked, voice rising. "I've always been fighting for you. Always! Since the moment you were born."

Margaret snorted and rolled her eyes. "Mhmm."

"The fact that our entire relationship has been one big fight is proof enough, don't you think?" Charlene continued. "If I didn't care, I would have given up a long time ago. But I've always tried. I've always worked to be the mother you needed me to be. Even now with you standing here attacking me, I'm trying. Even after I took in the son that you abandoned, I'm still trying."

"Don't bring Tyler into this!"

"He is a part of this!" Charlene shouted. "And he should be. He is *your son*, Margaret. And you left him on my doorstep with nothing more than a note and some clothes that didn't fit. I don't even know his birthday. I couldn't even be sure he was yours."

"I knew you'd know it was me," Margaret mumbled.

Charlene jabbed a finger in Margaret's direction. "Because I pay attention, and I care. And deep down, you know it. That's why you left Tyler with me."

"I left him with you because I was in a bind. That's it." Margaret top lip pulled up in a sneer. "I wouldn't have if I could have avoided it. But now I'm back, and I'm ready to take him with me again."

All of Charlene's worst theories confirmed. Margaret didn't trust her or respect her. Charlene had simply been a last resort. Her only option.

But that didn't matter anymore. It couldn't. Margaret had made her choice. Now, Charlene would make hers.

"No."

Margaret tilted her head to the side. "Excuse me?"

"No," Charlene repeated. "You aren't taking him with you."

"He's my son."

"The son you stood before a judge and said you didn't want. I'm not letting you leave with him."

"You can't keep him from me."

"Actually, I think I can," she said. "I have more legal claim to him than you do right now. And he isn't safe with you."

"What do you know about me?" Margaret demanded. "You don't know anything about my life. About whether I can take care of him."

"Look at you!" Charlene flung a hand in Margaret's direction. "You are bruised-up and rail thin. You look sick. You can't even take care of yourself, let alone a kid."

Margaret tightened her hold on her own torso. Almost like she could disappear if she squeezed herself hard enough.

As much as Charlene had been wanting to see her daughter, this wasn't how it was supposed to go. Maybe it would be for the best if she left. Maybe it would be easier for everyone if she stayed gone, too.

"Tyler is inside by himself," Charlene said. "I need to get in there, and I think it would be best if you left. He needs stability right now. You can't be that for him."

"Oh God, here we go again," Margaret groaned. "Please, tell me all the ways I'm failing. As if I haven't heard it from you enough in my lifetime."

"Don't be dramatic."

"I'm not," Margaret said. "You've never loved me for who I am. You were always trying to turn me into someone else."

Charlene stumbled back a step. "That isn't true."

"Isn't it, though? You hated my clothes and my make-up. I couldn't say anything to you without getting a lecture about how disrespectful I was or how I shouldn't gossip or do this or say that."

"I was trying to raise you." Charlene's voice came out in a whisper. "I was... I was teaching you how to be a person. That's all."

"It was more than that. You know it was," Margaret said. "Even when I tried to take Dad down to the beach the day before he died, you ran after us screaming about how I should be letting him rest. How it was too hot. I wanted to give him a nice day, and you ruined everything because you couldn't stand that it had been *my* idea to get him out of that stuffy room."

Charlene remembered the day well. Davy had been motionless for over twenty-four hours. She couldn't even figure out how Margaret had gotten him into the wheelchair by herself. But she had. And then she'd wheeled him down to the beach. Sand got in the gears and made the wheelchair almost impossible to push back up to the house.

"How could you be so irresponsible, Margaret?" she'd cried. "Your dad needs to rest. He needs to be monitored and looked after. He could have died."

Going into Davy's room and finding the bed empty had sent Charlene out of her mind with worry. When she'd found them on the beach, she'd lashed out at Margaret without thinking.

Almost half a decade stood between that moment and this one. But the look in Margaret's eyes hadn't changed one bit. One part loathing, one part shame. "You sent me up to my room." Margaret stared down at her shoes. "And then he died."

The air in Charlene's lungs forced its way out. She felt deflated. "Margaret, I'm… I'm sorry. I didn't mean—"

"Dad was the only one who never tried to change me. And then he was gone. I couldn't stay here anymore." Margaret looked back over her shoulder at the house. "I couldn't live with the memory of him around me all the time. And I couldn't stand your disappointment. It was easier to leave."

"I was not disappointed in you!"

"Yes, you were." Margaret wiped her forearm across her nose and sniffled. "And I can't even blame you. Because you're right."

Suddenly, Margaret's entire posture changed. She dropped her chin to her chest. Her shoulders sagged forward. And she began to cry. A shaking kind of sob that wracked her frail body.

Instinctively, Charlene crossed the distance between them and pulled Margaret into a hug. "You are not a disappointment."

"I'm messed up, Mom," Margaret said. "Really bad. I need help."

Charlene had been waiting for this moment for years. For the moment when her daughter would come home to her. When she'd finally tire of the lifestyle she was living and want something better for herself. When she'd stop playing the victim and take responsibility.

But never in her wildest dreams had Charlene thought it would happen like this.

"I'm sorry." Margaret sobbed into Charlene's shoulder. "I'm so sorry, Mom. For everything. For running away and leaving Tyler and—"

"It's fine," Charlene whispered as she smoothed down Margaret's hair. "It's okay. I can help you. You're home now."

Margaret sniffled. "I'll do whatever it takes. Rehab. Support groups. Whatever it takes to earn your trust. I can't... I can't keep going like this. I need help."

"I'll help," Charlene repeated. "I promise. We'll figure this out together."

Margaret wrapped her arms tightly around Charlene's middle and squeezed. She held Charlene like she was afraid to let go. Like she was worried her mom would disappear if she did.

But neither of them were going anywhere. Not this time. Not again.

16

THAT NIGHT AT CHARLENE'S HOUSE

When Annette came home that afternoon, there was a lot to explain.

"You're letting her stay here?" Annette asked. "In your house?"

"It's her house, too."

After five years, Charlene had been shocked at how natural it felt to have Margaret back at home. Things weren't normal, of course. And Charlene didn't even know if she wanted that. Normal for them was dysfunction. But having her daughter in her sights was... something.

"Not for the last five years," Annette whispered. "And what about Tyler? Do you think her being here is good for him? He's a little kid. He doesn't understand what is going on."

"I really don't know."

"He should be your first priority."

"I know. He is," Charlene said. Her first thought when she'd seen Margaret had been to send Tyler away, to deal with Margaret when he wasn't around. She wanted to save him any additional heartbreak. But she didn't think banishing Margaret would accomplish that. "Noah said that reunification is the main thing caseworkers hope for. I think it's what we should hope for, too."

Annette chewed on her lower lip. "Hope is one thing. We should hope for the best. But we can't confuse hope with expectations. I don't want to see you disappointed, Char."

"I'm being realistic about this," Charlene said. "But I'm going to do what I can to help both of them. Margaret is fragile right now. She needs me."

Margaret and Tyler were playing in the living room. She kept building a house out of sofa cushions that Tyler would stomp on and destroy, both of them laughing all the while.

"I think we need each other," Charlene continued softly. "She wants to do better."

Annette took a deep breath. "It's your house and your daughter and it's your decision. I just want to make sure you're thinking this through."

"My daughter is home. I'm not letting her leave again so easily."

Annette smiled softly and pulled Charlene in for a hug. "Okay then. I'm happy for you."

Margaret asked to put Tyler down for bed, and Charlene couldn't think of a reason for her not to. Plus, it seemed like a good sign that Margaret had *asked* in the first place. On some level, she recognized Charlene's boundaries around Tyler. Still…

"Will you make sure things run smoothly?" Charlene asked Annette. "Make sure Margaret actually puts him to sleep and doesn't mess with his schedule too much?"

"You don't trust her?"

"It's not that, it's… well, we just got to where he is only waking up once or twice every night. I don't want to ruin it."

Annette looked unconvinced. "Are you going somewhere?"

"For a walk." That was the easiest explanation. And it was true… in a way.

Annette waved a hand towards the door. "Sure thing. You go ahead. I can manage things here."

Charlene smiled in thanks. "And just in case you've forgotten, there are schools here where you could teach. You don't have to go back to Asheville if you don't want."

"Give it a rest," Annette laughed. "We both know you just want a free babysitter."

"That's part of it," Charlene admitted. "But I also want my sister around."

Annette smiled and waved a hand towards the door again. "Go on. Get out of here, you sap."

They'd had more than their fair share of emotional moments lately. Neither of them needed another one quite yet.

Charlene slipped on her sandals and, when Annette turned her back, grabbed her car keys. Once she was at the end of the front walk, Charlene pulled out her phone and dialed Noah's number.

Surprisingly, he answered on the third ring. "Hello?"

"Oh, hello. Hi," Charlene fumbled. "Sorry. I didn't think you'd—I expected your voicemail."

"I can hang up and you can call again if you'd rather."

Charlene couldn't tell if it was a joke or not. The usual good humor was gone from his voice.

"No, it's fine," she said. "This is better, actually. I want to talk to you. That's why I called."

"That's usually what a phone call implies," he drawled.

This was already so much harder than Charlene had expected. She took a deep, steadying breath before she continued. "I want to talk to you, Noah. Now, if possible. I told Annette I was going for a walk on the beach, but I can drive over to your place. Or if you're out, then—"

"I'm out. I'll just meet you at the beach," he said quickly. "I don't want to make a liar out of you."

It felt like something was being implied, but Noah hung up before Charlene could gather the courage to ask what it was. She had lied to him, in a way, yes. But not intentionally. Certainly not maliciously.

By the time Charlene navigated the dark beach path and kicked off her sandals in the sand, it was only a few minutes before a dark figure moved down the path towards her.

"It's me," Noah announced when he was still a good distance away. "I didn't want to scare you."

"I appreciate that." Charlene was already scared for a very different reason, though. Her hands felt sweaty, and she wiped her palms against the sides of her jeans. "Sorry to make you come out here."

"You didn't make me do anything." Noah stopped six feet away and shoved his hands in his jean pockets.

"Right. I didn't mean—I just—" Charlene shook her jumbled head. "Thanks for coming. And answering your phone."

"I thought it might be an emergency."

If he'd known what she really had in mind, would he have still answered his phone? Would he be standing in front of her right now? Charlene decided not to play that question out. She didn't want to know.

"Sit." Charlene dropped down into the sand and gestured to the spot next to her. "Or stand, I guess. But I'm going to sit."

Noah hesitated for a moment, then sat down next to her. Charlene thought she saw a flicker of amusement cross his features, but it could have been a trick of what little light there was. The sun had been down for half an hour, so the sky ahead of them was already a deep midnight blue.

"I didn't like how we left things," Charlene said finally.

"Me neither."

"Good. Well, not good. I'm just glad we agree. About how bad it was that we... disagreed."

A heavy hand landed on Charlene's shoulder. She looked over, and Noah's brows were pinched together in either sympathy or concern. Maybe both. "Relax, please," he said. "You're so nervous it's making me nervous."

Charlene groaned. "I'm sorry. I just don't know how to talk to you when you aren't being nice to me."

"I'm being nice," he said.

Charlene thought about it for a second and then agreed. "Actually, that's sort of true. You're being... neutral. Usually, you are making fun of me or making snide comments or trying to make me blush. I don't know how to react to *this* Noah."

"For the record, I never tried to make you blush. But I'm sorry. I'm not really in a teasing mood."

"Don't apologize," Charlene said. "I should be the one apologizing, okay? I brain-dumped everything I was thinking on you without any context or setup. It was a lot to take in. It's no wonder you got mad."

"I didn't get mad because you dumped your thoughts and feelings on me," he said. "I got mad because I didn't like what your thoughts and feelings were. There's a difference."

Charlene nodded. "I know. You're right. I'm sorry for that, too. Despite outward appearances, I'm not perfect, you know?"

At that, Noah finally smiled. "Shocker."

A flicker of hope lit in her chest, but Charlene tried not to give in to it. Not yet.

"I've never been good at the whole mothering thing. I loved my daughter, but raising her never came naturally. And I've always felt like I failed her. I didn't want to fail Tyler, too."

"Why do you think you'd fail him?" he asked. "From what I've seen, you are a natural. You two have an obvious bond. Even after only a few weeks."

Charlene's heart twisted at that. She felt it, too—the bond. The love that had already bloomed between them. It was like Charlene had been there with him since the very beginning.

"I was talking to Annette earlier that afternoon, and I got to thinking… maybe I'm trying to somehow correct my mistakes with Margaret. Maybe I'm using Tyler as a replacement for her."

"That's not what you're doing."

"Are you sure?" Charlene turned to Noah. "Because I for one am not so sure. I'm not sure at all. But I am sure that if there is any chance I'm being selfish with Tyler, I'd rather let another deserving family take care of him. Because he deserves to be loved for who he is and nothing else."

Noah reached out and curled both of his hands around Charlene's. "The fact that you can say that means you love him for who he is. The very fact that you're worried about failing him means that you won't."

"You don't know that."

"Believe me," he continued, "I've seen enough bad caregivers to know. The truly bad ones have no idea they're doing a bad job. The best ones worry incessantly."

Charlene chuckled softly. "That actually makes sense."

"Only people who care about doing a good job worry that they aren't," he said. "And adopting a kid is huge. It's normal to freak out and doubt yourself. But the only way you'd fail Tyler is if you gave up without ever really trying."

Charlene sighed. "I wished you'd told me that years ago. It would have saved me a lot of guilt and heartache with Margaret. And with Tyler."

"I wish I'd known you years ago so I could have told you." Noah gently released Charlene's hands and turned towards the dark water.

He didn't hate her. And right now, that was enough.

"Well," she continued, "as good as that advice is, it doesn't really matter anymore."

His attention snapped back to her. "What does that mean?"

"Tyler's mom is back," she said. "Margaret is home. She came back this afternoon."

"She's back? Like, for good? Like, she came back for Tyler?"

"That's what she said. I don't have a reason not to believe her."

Noah's head bobbed side to side in uncertainty. "I mean... it seems like you have a lot of reasons not to believe her. She went to a judge and asked not to be his mom anymore. What changed?"

"She did," Charlene said. "Margaret admitted to me that she messed up. She said she is willing to do whatever it takes to earn my trust and to earn Tyler's trust. She wants to do this."

"And you think that's a good idea?"

"You sound like Annette," Charlene said. "Isn't reunification what you hope for? That's what you told me."

He nodded. "Well, yeah, but... It's only what we hope for when it's the right call. And after a lengthy process of the biological parents proving themselves worthy. You can't just hand Tyler back over to her and expect things to be instantly better. That's not how human beings work."

"I don't expect that. And neither does she. She knows it will take time."

Noah took a deep breath and planted his hands in the sand behind him. "So you won't be adopting him, then?"

"I don't think so. Not if Margaret is back."

The admission brought with it a deep ache in Charlene's chest. But not the same way it had hurt knowing he'd be going to a different family. This was a bittersweet ache.

"And there's still time for things to change."

"With Margaret, you mean?"

"Yeah. You know, in case she... doesn't stay."

"She'll stay."

"I hope so."

"She will," Charlene insisted. "In all the years of us fighting, she never apologized to me. Not once—until today. That means something."

Noah nodded. "Whatever is best for Tyler and you, that's what I want."

Charlene's heart leapt in desperate hope. "Thank you. That means a lot."

"And I mean it," he said. "I know our fight was... well, it wasn't my proudest moment. I just think you and Tyler make so much sense. Seeing you together—it's something special, Charlene."

"I know it is. And I'll still be his grandma," she said. "Margaret can be his mom, and I can spend all of my time spoiling him the way grandmas are supposed to. It could be really great."

"You're a great grandma." Noah chuckled. "Well, not a literal great-grandma, but a wonderful grandma. The world's best."

Charlene couldn't help but picture Noah as a grandpa. The silly jokes he would make. The way Tyler would adore him. She was dangerously far ahead of herself, but still, the image was nice.

"And you can still be his 'Handsome Noah,'" she said. "If you want to be. Part of his life, I mean."

Noah turned to her with a raised brow. "He did call me handsome that day, didn't he? I'm guessing he didn't come up with that nickname on his own."

Charlene laughed. "I didn't start it, but it is an apt description."

"Oh, Charlene." Noah swatted a bashful hand in the air. "Now you're the one making me blush."

The last of Charlene's nerves slipped away. She and Noah were going to be okay.

Charlene plucked Noah's hand out of the air. When their intertwined fingers fell back against the still-warm sand, she felt a peace she hadn't known in a long time.

"I'll be in his life no matter what he wants to call me," Noah said. Then he leaned over and nudged Charlene's elbow with his. "I'll be in your life, too. Though, I would prefer if you referred to me exclusively as 'Handsome Noah.'"

Charlene tipped her head back and laughed. "In your dreams."

"My dreams have come true before." He winked, she grinned, waves crashed. Things were good.

17

LATE NIGHT AT CHARLENE'S HOUSE

Charlene and Noah sat on the beach for a long time, talking and laughing about nothing and everything. And as she walked back up the path towards her house, Charlene felt like the pieces of her life were finally coming together.

She had her sister back. She had her daughter back. And on top if it all, she'd gained Tyler and Noah. Charlene had everything she ever wanted plus some, and she didn't know if her fragile old heart could handle all the love she was experiencing.

A perma-smile still stretched her face to the point of being painful as she quietly tiptoed across the squeaky wooden porch, so as not to wake anyone, and turned the knob on the front door.

From the outside, all of the windows were dark. She figured everyone was asleep. But as she stepped into the entryway, she saw a flashlight beam dancing across the floor. It was coming from the direction of the dining room.

Her first thought was a burglar, and she wished she'd kept the solid bronze umbrella stand next to the door so she'd at least have something to swing if the criminal tried to come at her. But it was packed away in the basement now, and Charlene was defenseless.

So she stood frozen in the doorway. Should she run back outside and call Noah? Call the cops? Call for somebody, anybody to help? Or did she charge in and protect her family?

Before she could choose, the decision was taken away from her.

Charlene heard something roll across the table and land on the floor with a thud. "Shoot."

Immediately, the hairs on the back of Charlene's neck raised. Even in a whispered hiss, she knew that voice. She'd recognize it anywhere.

Charlene padded softly down the hallway towards the dining room. Next to the table, a thin figure stood. She had the flashlight on her cellphone turned on. The light illuminated the contents of Charlene's purse, which were spread across the table. Her expired bottle of pepper spray was laying on the floor where it had fallen just a moment ago.

"What are you doing?" Charlene would have rather turned the corner and seen a thief in a ski mask standing over her purse. Heck, she'd rather have seen the Grim Reaper himself.

Instead, she saw this.

She saw *her*.

Margaret jumped so hard at the sound of Charlene's voice that she dropped her phone on the table. The crash was like dynamite going off in the quiet house. She scrambled to pick it up before she turned to Charlene, eyes wide.

Charlene shook her head. Angry tears already burned. "What are you doing?" she croaked again. She already knew the answer.

"I thought you were asleep," Margaret said with a nervous laugh. "I was thinking about going out, but I don't have a house key. So I thought I'd grab yours."

Charlene stared at the daughter she hardly recognized anymore. "My keys are hanging in the kitchen. On the hook next to the garage door. Where they've always been."

"Oh, duh." Margaret slapped her forehead and stepped away from the table. "I can't believe I forgot that. I've been away longer than I thought."

Charlene squeezed her eyes closed for a second and took a deep breath. "What are you doing, Margaret? I want the truth."

"I told you," Margaret said. "Your keys. I wanted to go out. Maybe get a drink. I can have a drink, can't I? Or does Mommy still enforce curfew around here?"

The question dripped with sarcastic acid. It reminded Charlene of teenage Margaret. Almost as if no time had passed at all, which felt especially true, considering what she was looking at.

The morning after Margaret had left, Charlene had found her purse in a similar state. No note, no explanation of where Margaret was going. Just an empty wallet.

"Of course you can," Charlene said. "You're an adult."

Margaret lifted her chin. "Then why are you treating me like a kid?"

"Why are you treating me like I'm stupid?" Anger prickled under Charlene's skin. "I know what you're doing."

"And what is that?" Margaret crossed her arms. She was waiting for her mom to say it. Forcing Charlene to accuse her so she could deny it and play the victim. Charlene knew the game well.

"Let's not pretend we don't both already know you were stealing from me." Margaret gasped and recoiled, but Charlene continued before she could say anything. "Were you going to take some money and go get a drink? Because I would have given you some spending money if you needed it."

"*Spending money?* You really do think I'm a kid, don't you?"

"You're the one who was going through my purse, Margaret! I'm trying to figure out why." Charlene spun around and flipped on the light switch. They both blinked against the sudden brightness in the room. Seeing the contents of her purse spread across the table in full light felt like seeing a body lying on a morgue table. There was something cold and unnatural about it.

Margaret crossed her arms and leaned away from the crime scene. Her lips were pressed together so tightly they were white.

"If you weren't looking for money for a drink, then what? Were you planning to empty my wallet and disappear again?"

The way Margaret eyes narrowed told Charlene everything she needed to know.

When Margaret was ten, she liked to watch legal dramas with Davy. Syndicated shows set in small towns with a world-class detective. From that, she learned what "pleading the fifth" meant, and she proceeded to make extremely regular use of it.

When Charlene found a bucket of spilled paint in the garage? *"I plead the fifth."*

When someone swiped all the frosting off of the backside of Davy's birthday cake one hour before his party? *"I plead the fifth."*

And each time she spoke those magic words, Margaret's shoulders would set and her eyes would narrow as she stared Charlene down.

She had the same expression on now. Charlene felt like she might be sick.

"What happened to going to rehab and getting treatment? What happened to earning back my trust?" Charlene whispered. Margaret didn't say anything. She just turned her head away like she was bored. "That was only a few hours ago. What changed since then?"

Again, Margaret wouldn't respond.

So Charlene stepped forward and raised her voice. "What changed since then, Margaret?"

Her daughter's top lip curled. "Not a damn thing."

The reality Charlene had been trying to avoid washed over her all at once with those four little words. Margaret had been lying. Since the moment she'd stepped out of the shadows on the front porch, everything out of her mouth had been a lie.

The crying. The apology. The promises. All of it had been empty. Meaningless.

Margaret had pulled out her classic trick. The same one she pulled on Davy the night he confronted her about her underage partying. The same one she pulled on Annette when she showed up at her house crying and begging her aunt not to tell Charlene where she was.

Even knowing everything she knew about her daughter, Charlene had fallen for it yet again. Hook, line, and sinker.

Because she'd wanted to believe it. Because it was easier to be hopeful than to be rational.

"You lied to me."

"Ditto," Margaret snapped.

Charlene shook her head. "What does that mean?"

"Do you really think I buy your crap story about Dad?" she spat. "Or that twenty-three years of you barely tolerating me could be washed away in one afternoon?"

"People can change. Or… that's what I thought. What I hoped."

"*You* haven't changed," Margaret snarled. "You're still hoping I'll magically turn into someone else. Into the perfect daughter you always wanted. Which is why it was so easy to lie to you."

There was almost a sense of pride in Margaret's voice, like she was proud of herself, happy that she'd tricked her own mother into thinking she wanted to reconcile. Charlene felt like she was looking at the fun house version of her daughter. A distorted image warped and twisted by misplaced anger and trauma. It was hard to look at her at all.

"You lied about everything?" Charlene asked. "None of it was true?"

Margaret shrugged and her mouth tilted up into a half-smirk. "What do you think?"

Had any question ever hurt more? Charlene nearly reeled from it like a physical blow to the chest. "Get out," she gritted. "Now."

Margaret raised a brow. "You're kicking me out? But Mommy, I just got back."

She was mocking her with that simpering little girl voice. Charlene had been mocked enough already. She couldn't stand anymore.

"Get out now, Margaret. Or I'll call the police." Her voice shook with anger and a sadness unlike anything she'd ever known. It felt like a pit was yawning open inside of her. Like all the light she'd managed to find in the last few weeks was winking out, bit by bit by bit.

"Call the police if you want. Me and Tyler won't be here when they arrive."

"You can't take him with you." Instinctively, Charlene moved to block Margaret's path to the stairs. "He is staying here."

"He's my son!"

"A son you don't even want," Charlene snapped. "You left him on my front porch. The only reason you came back today was for money."

Margaret's eyes narrowed again. "Don't you—"

"You came back here because you only care about yourself. Not Tyler. You never cared about Tyler."

"But you do, don't you, Mom?" Margaret accused. "You care about him way more than you ever cared about me."

"You're wrong about that, Margaret. But I know you won't let me convince you otherwise. And that's the only reason you want him, isn't it? Because I do care about him and you want to make me miserable." Charlene shook her head. "I'm not going to let you control any of our lives. Not anymore, Margaret. From this moment on, you stay away from us."

"There is no *us*," Margaret said. "There is you and then there's my son. And my son is coming with me."

Charlene may not have had her umbrella stand or any other weapon, but she knew in that moment that she would fight her own daughter tooth and nail to protect Tyler. No matter what happened. Because he wasn't her second chance at raising a child and he wasn't a replacement for Margaret. He was just the most beautiful little boy she'd ever known, and she'd die to protect him.

"That boy is mine," Charlene said, her voice slow and low and clear. "And I'll do whatever it takes to protect him from anyone who wants to hurt him. Including you."

Charlene stared at her daughter. Her once-hazel eyes looked dimmer now than they ever had before. Finally, Margaret shoved her phone in her pocket and shrugged. "Fine. What do I care? It's not like I wanted him in the first place. He was an accident. On top of drugs, you can add 'unwanted teen pregnancy' to the long list of ways you failed me."

A few weeks ago—maybe even a few hours ago—the comment would have sliced Charlene open. Instead, the words glanced off, leaving barely a scratch.

"Use the back door." Charlene pointed. "And don't come back."

Margaret rolled her lips together for a second, no doubt trying to see if there was a way out of this situation. If she could play her cards right and work this all for her own selfish good. But as soon as she realized the jig was up, she turned on her heel and marched through the back door.

The wooden door bounced off the wall. Charlene stared at the dark opening her daughter had disappeared through for a few seconds.

Then she walked across the room and gently closed it. The *CLUNK* of the lock sliding into place was the most final sound she'd ever heard.

18

LATE NIGHT AT CHARLENE'S HOUSE

Charlene heard the familiar sound of little footsteps on the stairs before she heard his voice.

"Where's Mommy going?"

She didn't want to turn around. Didn't want to have to look a precious little boy in the face and tell him his mommy wasn't coming back. But Charlene had to. Because she loved Tyler. And because there was no one else to do it for her.

She turned around and tried to smile, but quickly gave up. Tyler was wearing his short-sleeved dinosaur onesie pajamas. His bare feet stuck out of the thick green cuffs at the bottom. Framed by the hallway doorframe, he looked so small. So fragile.

Charlene knelt down and held out her arms. Tyler ran to them immediately and looked up at her. "Did Mommy leave?"

"She did," Charlene said, snuggling him close. "She had to go."

He frowned. "Was she mad?"

"She wasn't mad at you. Who could ever be mad at you?" Charlene kissed his cheek. He smelled like his lavender bath wash and lotion. It was quickly becoming her favorite smell.

"But she had a mad voice. So did you."

Charlene took a breath. "We were both angry. But not with you. I promise."

That seemed to comfort him slightly. "Is she coming back?" he asked. "She was only here today. She said we could go to the beach tomorrow."

Earlier that afternoon, Margaret and Tyler had been making plans. "Me and Grandma went to a fish zoo with big pools and ate pancakes," he'd said excitedly.

"The aquarium," Charlene had translated. "We went to the aquarium."

Tyler had grabbed onto Margaret's hand. "We can go to the 'quarium tomorrow?"

"Maybe the beach instead?" Margaret had suggested. "I haven't been in the ocean in forever. We could play in the water. How about that?"

Tyler's eyes had lit up with excitement.

What hurt Charlene right then, as she held her grandson close while his mother put step after step between her and him, was that Margaret had said those words even though she already knew she intended to leave.

A mother's love could forgive many things, and Lord knows Charlene's love certainly had. But this would be hard to forgive. Setting up a three-year-old for disappointment was… it was cruel.

"I'm sorry, honey, but I don't think Mommy is going to be here tomorrow. She had to leave, so she can't go to the beach."

Tyler's face instantly fell. "But she said… We were gonna build a sand castle. I was gonna show her the turtle nests."

"It was a good plan." Charlene smoothed a hand over his back. "But she had to leave."

Tears welled in his hazel eyes. "She didn't give a cuddle before she left. Or a kiss."

Charlene hugged him tighter. "I'm sorry, buddy."

The emotion overwhelmed him slowly. His chin quivered, his shoulders sagged, and then he was leaning against Charlene's shoulder. His entire body shook with tears. Charlene had never wanted to take someone's pain away so badly before.

"You know I love you, don't you?" she whispered. "You know you're my favorite boy in the whole world?"

He nodded his head weakly.

"We can still go to the beach. Just the two of us. We can look for the turtles and play in the water and—"

He sat bolt upright and looked at her. "Right now?'

"*No*" sat on the end of Charlene's tongue. It was late and dark. Tyler should have been asleep for hours already. Plus, Charlene was exhausted. From the surprise of her daughter showing up, from her conversation with Noah, from the fight with Margaret that followed. The day had been an emotional rollercoaster, and all she wanted to do was curl up in bed.

But she couldn't quite bring herself to say it. Not after everything Tyler had just witnessed. Not after everything he'd already been through. Not when Charlene knew the weeks and months and years ahead would be difficult for him.

She didn't want him to look back on this night and think about his mom and his Grandma fighting. Charlene couldn't wipe away the memory of Margaret and what she'd said, but she could compete with it. She could give Tyler something else worth remembering.

So she nodded. "Sure. Right now. Do you want to go right now?'

Tyler jumped off her lap and lifted his hands in the air. "Yes!"

"Then let's go."

Charlene grabbed flashlights from the hallway closet and the two of them set off into the darkness, hand in hand. Usually, Tyler wandered ahead down the beach path. He'd put space between himself and Charlene and then wait for her to catch up. But tonight, he stuck close to her side. His eyes were wide as he looked ahead on the dark path.

"Is it nighttime?" he asked.

"It is. It's very late. Way past your bedtime."

Tyler grinned mischievously. Tomorrow night's bedtime would likely be a fight, but that was a problem for future Charlene to worry about. Right now, she was just thrilled to see his smiling face.

Clouds had covered the moon earlier in the evening, but now the sky was clear. When Charlene and Tyler made it down to the sand, the full moon's mirror image reflected off the water and lit up the night twice as brightly. They could see the entire beach washed in luminescent shades of white.

Tyler took off his sandals and pushed his pajama pants up as high as they would go on his calves before he ran straight for the dark surf. Charlene stayed close behind. The bottoms of her jeans disappeared in the water, but she couldn't bring herself to care.

So much of her life had been spent worrying for the next moment. She'd never been good at being in the present. But with Tyler, she wanted to be different. Right now, she wanted to be nowhere else but here.

They splashed in the water for a few minutes before Tyler turned back towards the beach and squinted. He stood still long enough that Charlene walked over to him and followed his gaze.

"What is it, bud?"

He pointed to the sand. "What is that?"

The moon offered some light, but hardly enough for Charlene's old eyes to see what Tyler's could. She grabbed the flashlight out of her pocket and shined it towards the sand. As soon as the beam hit the ground, she yelped in surprise.

"Turtles!" Tyler chirped.

He scrambled out of the water and made his way towards the turtle exodus. Wet sand sucked at her feet as Charlene hurried after him.

"Wait, wait, honey," she said. She grabbed his hand and pulled him out of the line of turtles and up the beach to where the nest was. The caution tape and poles were still around the nest, but the sand was giving way as baby turtles no bigger than Charlene's palm scurried out of the ground, joining their siblings on the long, fraught trip to the water.

"They hatched!" Tyler knelt down a few feet from the parade of turtles making their way across the sand. "Where are they going?"

Charlene knelt down beside him. "To the ocean, remember? That's where they're going to live now."

"They don't live in the nest?"

"They are born in the nest, but they belong in the ocean," she explained.

Tyler tilted his head to one side. "The ocean is their new home?"

"Yeah, they're going to live in the ocean now."

"For forever?" Tyler asked.

Charlene paused. For years, she'd liked to watch the turtles hatch because they gave her hope. Hope that somewhere out there was the chance at a new start. Even if Charlene never found one of her own, new beginnings still happened all around her. They were possible.

But now, with her arm around Tyler's back as they watched the turtles scuttle into the ocean, Charlene knew she'd found her own fresh start. She intended to make the most of it.

She pressed a kiss to Tyler's temple and smiled. "Yes, darling," she whispered. "For forever."

EPILOGUE: NINE MONTHS LATER

The sound of water dripping and splattering on the wood floor caught Charlene's attention. She jogged to the base of the stairs.

"What are you doing up there?"

After a few seconds of hesitation, Tyler answered. "I was just... I was just... My turtle needed a bath."

Charlene took the stairs two at a time and walked into the bathroom to find Tyler elbow deep in a completely full sink. Water was splashing over the sides, collecting on the counter and the floor. His favorite stuffed turtle, Sheldon, was submerged under water. A few bubbles came out of the poor creature's felt eyeballs.

"Sheldon just had a bath the other day," Charlene said as she hurriedly turned off the water and pulled the plug on the sink. "What if we wipe up this water and throw him in the dryer?"

Tyler yanked the turtle out of the water and held it to his chest, completely soaking his shirt. "But he's scared of the dryer."

"Don't you want him to be able to come to your party?"

Tyler's brows pinched in concern. He looked down at Sheldon's soggy face for a few seconds and then sighed. "Yes."

"Then you wipe up the water, Birthday Boy, and I'll go dry off Sheldon." Charlene plucked Sheldon out of Tyler's hand and kissed Tyler on the head.

When she got back downstairs, Noah was still standing at the stove where she'd left him. He had on one of Charlene's floral aprons, which reached her knees when she wore it but hardly grazed the top of his thighs.

"Everything okay up there?" he asked.

She held up the dripping Sheldon. "Just a pre-party bath for Mr. Sheldon. I'm going to throw him in the dryer."

"Better be quick about it or Sheldon will miss this culinary masterpiece I'm whipping up."

Charlene peeked over Noah's shoulder. "Oh, yes. Macaroni and cheese grilled cheese. I'll alert the foodies of the world."

"Watch it!" Noah laughed and elbowed her in the side. "You're the one who let Tyler pick the menu for his party. And I'm doing my best with it. We have three different kinds of cheeses in here. And I bought the bread fresh from a bakery this morning. Prepare your tastebuds."

Charlene stretched onto her toes and pecked his cheek lightly. "Thank you."

Noah bit back a smile. "Of course. Anything for—Tyler. For Tyler."

"Of course. For Tyler." Charlene bit back a smile of her own.

She tossed her grandson's stuffed turtle into the dryer, just as the man of the hour moseyed down the stairs in his wet shirt to help with the last of the party setup. It was hardly a "party" in the classical sense. Tyler wasn't in school yet and didn't have many friends his own age, so it was just Noah, Charlene, and Annette on the guest list. Still, he'd excitedly settled on the theme of "turtles"—no surprises there—and they were all thrilled to be able to celebrate him.

As Tyler helped Charlene tape a "Pin the Shell on the Turtle" game to the wall, he turned to her. "My mom won't be here?"

It had been nine months since Margaret had walked out the back door and five months since she'd officially signed away her parental rights, sight unseen, but Tyler still asked about her. He probably always would. Charlene did her best not to shy away from any of his questions.

"No, she won't be here," she said. "Just me and Aunt Net and Noah."

"And Sheldon?"

Charlene smiled. "As soon as he's dry."

Suddenly, the sound of footsteps thundered down the steps. "Sorry, sorry!" Annette called. "I know I'm late."

Annette was in a green summer dress with matching eyeshadow and a large silver turtle necklace hanging from around her neck. She was struggling to carry an abnormally large present in her arms.

"How can you be late when you live upstairs?" Charlene teased.

Annette dropped the present on the gift table at the base of the stairs and then bent to kiss the top of Tyler's head. "Well, first, the wrapping paper and I had a bit of a disagreement. It took the first few rounds but I won in the end. Second, I had to wait for the water to warm up before I could take a shower."

"That wouldn't happen if you showered earlier in the morning."

Charlene and Annette may have been sisters, but they couldn't have had two more different morning routines. Charlene was up and at 'em before the sun rose, but Annette liked to roll out of bed at the last possible minute. She gave herself just enough time to shower, eat an on-the-go breakfast, and make it to work before she was late.

Charlene had been trying to change her sister's ways with little success.

"It wouldn't happen if this old house had a bigger water heater," Annette argued.

She had a point there. Back when Charlene had been trying to sell the house, an inspector had told her she needed a new water heater. But now that selling was off the table and she and Annette split the monthly mortgage, she planned to replace the water heater only when it broke and not a day sooner.

"Feel free to move out if you want," Charlene said. "You're an 'in-demand' teacher, remember?"

Annette wrapped her arm around her sister's shoulder and squeezed. "Not a chance. You're stuck with me!"

For weeks before Annette was supposed to head back to Asheville and her private school teaching job, Charlene had tried to get Annette to stay on the Isle of Palms with her. Every time, Annette rebuffed the suggestion without much consideration. Until finally, she'd walked through the front door and announced she was staying.

"You're staying?" Charlene had asked. "*Staying here?*"

Annette had nodded with a wide grin stretched across her face. "I just signed a contract as a speech therapist for the school district. I'm staying."

"I'm sorry… what? You said you didn't want to quit your old job!"

Annette had shrugged. "I lied. I didn't want to get my hopes up about staying if I couldn't find a new job in time. Or get your hopes up. I know how much you'd miss me."

She'd been right about that. Charlene hadn't at all been ready to see her sister leave. And now, nine months later, she still wasn't ready. After five years apart, it was nice to spend so much time together. They were closer than ever, and Charlene had zero regrets.

Except for the thing that brought Annette back to the island in the first place, of course. She hated knowing her sister was hurting and there was nothing she could do about it. Especially since, aside from angry mumblings under Annette's breath from time to time, her soon-to-be-ex-husband Frederick was a strictly off-limits topic. Charlene didn't see how she could help Annette if they couldn't talk through her feelings.

"I'm starting new," Annette would say whenever Charlene tried to mention Frederick in conversation. "There's no need to bring up my old baggage when I have such shiny, lovely new baggage right here."

"Are Tyler and I the baggage in this analogy?" Charlene would ask.

At that point, Annette would usually change the subject, and the topic of Frederick and his mistress and their new baby would fade once again into the background.

"But now that I'm finally here," Annette said, "it's time to party!"

Tyler jumped up and down with excitement. "We can eat cake now?"

"Not before we eat mac n' cheese grilled cheeses." Noah came in holding a platter of steaming sandwiches.

Annette nodded in agreement. "Sandwiches first, then we can finally taste-test our cake."

Tyler had insisted on helping make his birthday cake, and he'd also insisted it be s'mores-flavored. Annette pulled out all the stops with graham cracker-infused cake sponge, chocolate ganache filling, and marshmallow fluff frosting. Charlene's kitchen had been a sticky, chocolatey mess by the time they were done, but the cake smelled so good that she couldn't bring herself to care.

After sandwiches and cake, they opened presents. Tyler tore through wrapping paper with a vengeance to reveal new crabbing and fishing gear from Noah, a turtle backpack full of coloring books and crayons from Charlene, and a giant glass aquarium from Annette.

When Tyler opened the aquarium and found the inside empty, he turned to Annette with a confused smile. "Thank you?"

Annette cackled. "You're sweet, but that's just the first part of the gift. The second part, we have to go get together."

His eyes widened. "What is it?"

"Well," Annette said, "I was thinking it was about time you got your own pet."

"Annette!" Charlene warned. They hadn't discussed this at all. "What did you do?"

"He's a responsible young man and it's time he had something to look after." Annette leaned over and lowered her voice. "And I'll help him take care of it, don't worry."

"It?" Charlene asked. "Define 'it,' please."

Tyler was bouncing on his heels now. "What is it?"

"After your nap, I thought we could go to the pet store and buy— drumroll please... a turtle!" Annette announced.

Just as the words left her mouth, Tyler hurled himself at her and wrapped his arms around her neck. "Thank you, Aunt Net!"

Annette gave Charlene an apologetic smile over Tyler's shoulder and squeezed the little boy tightly. "You are so welcome, buddy. Happy birthday!"

"Can I go to nap now?" Tyler asked.

"Is the birthday boy asking for a nap?" Noah asked as they all laughed.

"I'm guessing it has a lot to do with what he gets to do *after* he naps," Charlene said.

Tyler nodded in confirmation. "I need to hurry and sleep. So I can get a turtle."

"That you do," Annette agreed. "Well, if there are no more presents to unwrap, then I'd be happy to tuck you in. Is that okay, Grandma?"

Charlene gave them the thumbs up. "Fine by me!"

As soon as they were gone, Noah chuckled. "You're about to be the proud owner of a turtle."

"Oh no, I most certainly am not! That's all Annette's responsibility," Charlene protested.

Noah laughed and then got up and crossed the room. He pulled a folder out of the backpack he'd brought with him that morning. "Well, maybe I have something that will be a little more exciting for you."

Charlene frowned. "It isn't my birthday."

"No, but I thought you deserved a little something anyway." He handed her the folder and tipped his head. "Open it."

Charlene slid the first sheet of paper out of the folder, and immediately, her heart stuttered. She knew what these were.

"I just got the go-ahead yesterday before I left work," Noah said. "I wanted to surprise you with them."

Charlene clapped a hand over her mouth. Tears were already welling in her eyes, making it hard to read the document. She only needed to read the heading, though.

Report of Adoption.

He nudged her shoulder. "Earth to Charlene, are you still with me? Are you excited?"

Tears slid down Charlene's cheeks, and she couldn't speak. So instead, she turned to Noah and kissed him.

He froze for only a second before he pulled her close and kissed her back. When they broke apart, he smiled down at her. "That was a long time coming."

Charlene nodded in agreement and then held up the adoption papers. "So were these."

"Maybe things are finally starting to fit together," he suggested.

Charlene leaned into him and sighed. "It sure seems that way."

They sat like that for a few more minutes until Annette came down the stairs. When she saw Noah and Charlene snuggled together on the floor, she smirked. "Sorry to interrupt."

"You're not. Actually, I have great news." All Charlene had to do was hold up the papers for Annette to understand what they meant.

"You can finally adopt Tyler?"

Charlene nodded, and Annette knelt down and hugged her sister tightly. "Char, I'm so happy for you. And for Tyler! Congratulations!"

"Thank you." Charlene swiped at her watery eyes. "I know it's what is best for him. And that's what matters."

They decided to celebrate the milestone by cutting off a few more pieces of the amazing s'mores cake. One slice in, however, there was a loud knock on the front door.

Annette turned towards the entryway with a frown. "Who could that be? They're going to wake Tyler up!" She jogged out of the kitchen and down the hall.

Noah sighed. "She took the cake-cutting knife with her."

They were both waiting in the kitchen for Annette to return and finish dishing out the cake, when suddenly, there was a loud, metallic clatter.

"What was that?" Charlene hurried out of the kitchen. Down the stretch of the hallway, she had a clear shot of Annette standing in the doorway. Her hands were limp at her sides. The cake knife wobbled on the floor at her feet.

"Annette?" Charlene called. "What is it?"

Annette didn't speak. Didn't move. She just stood there motionless, silhouetted by the door.

Charlene walked slowly down the hallway. "Annette, who is at the—?"

Before she could finish her question, Annette finally pushed the door further open and stepped to the side. It took Charlene's eyes a moment to adjust, but when they did, she suddenly understood her sister's reaction.

Standing on the porch in a pair of tan dockers with a dozen roses in his hands was Annette's ex-husband, Frederick.

He smiled at Charlene over Annette's shoulder and then turned his eyes back to his ex-wife. He held out the flowers to her. "I missed you, Annie."

Check out THE BEACH DATE, Book 2 in the Sunny Isle of Palms series, to find out what happens next!
The Beach Date

SNEAK PREVIEW OF NO HOME LIKE NANTUCKET

If you loved **The Beach Baby***, you'll fall head over heels for the Benson family in my beloved Sweet Island Inn series, set on the gorgeous island of Nantucket.*

Take a sneak preview below of Book 1 in the series, NO HOME LIKE NANTUCKET.

∼

NO HOME LIKE NANTUCKET:
A Sweet Island Inn Novel (Book 1)

Nantucket was their paradise—until reality came barging in.

An unexpected pregnancy.

A marriage on the rocks.

A forbidden workplace romance.

And a tragedy no one could have seen coming.

Take a trip to Nantucket's Sweet Island Inn and follow along as Mae Benson and her children—the Wall Street queen Eliza, stay-at-home mom Holly, headstrong chef Sara, and happy-go-lucky fisherman Brent—face the hardest summer of their lives.

Love, loss, heartbreak, hope—it's all here and more. Can the Benson family find a way to forgive themselves and each other? Or will their grief be too much to overcome?

Find out in **NO HOME LIKE NANTUCKET.**

Click here to start reading now!

❧

Chapter One: Mae

Mae Benson never ever slept in.

For each of the one thousand, two hundred, and eleven days that she'd lived at 114 Howard Street, Nantucket, Massachusetts, she'd gotten up with the dawn and started her morning the second her eyes opened. It wasn't because she was a busybody, or compulsive, or obsessive. On the contrary, snoozing for a while was tempting. Her bed was soft this morning. The first fingers of springtime sunlight had barely begun to peek in through the gauzy curtains that hung over the window. And she was in that perfect sleeping position—warm but not too warm, wrapped up but not too tightly.

But force of habit could sometimes be awfully hard to break. So, being careful to make as little noise as possible, she slid out from underneath the comforter, tucked her feet into the fuzzy slippers she'd received for her sixtieth birthday last year, and rose.

Her husband, Henry, always called her his little hummingbird. He'd even bought her a beautiful handblown hummingbird ornament for Christmas last year from a glassblower down by the wharf. It had jade-green wings, little amethysts for eyes, and a patch of ruby red on its chest. She loved how it caught and refracted the winter sunbeams, and she always made sure to put it on a limb of the tree where it could see the snow falling outdoors.

"Flitting around the house, are we?" Henry would say, laughing, every time he came downstairs from their master bedroom to find Mae buzzing from corner to corner. She would just laugh and shake her head. He could make fun of her all he wanted, but the fact remained that each of the little projects she had running at all times around the house required love and care from the moment the day began.

She ran through the list in her head as she moved silently around the bedroom getting dressed for the day. She needed to water the plants on the living room windowsill, the ones that her daughter, Sara, had sent from her culinary trip to Africa and made her mother promise to keep alive until she could retrieve them on her next visit. Crane flowers, with their gorgeous mix of orange- and blue-bladed leaves; desert roses, with their soft blush of red fading into the purest white; and her favorites, the fire lilies, that looked just like a flickering flame.

She had to check on the batch of marshmallow fluff fudge—a Mae Benson specialty—that she'd left to set in the freezer overnight. Her friend Lola, who lived down the street, had just twisted her ankle badly a few days prior and was laid up at home with a boot on her leg. Mae didn't know much about ankle injuries, but she had a lot of hands-on experience with fudge, so she figured she'd offer what she knew best.

She should also start coffee for Henry—lots of cream and sugar, as always. Henry had an outing planned that morning with Brent to go check on some fishing spots they'd been scheming over for the last few weeks. Mae knew he was excited about the trip. He'd been exhibiting trademark Happy Henry behavior all week long—eyes lighting up with that mischievous twinkle, hands rubbing together like an evil mastermind, and the way that he licked the corner of his lips, like he could already taste the salt air that hung on the wind and feel the bouncing of the boat as it raced through the waves.

Just before she turned to leave the bedroom and start her day, she looked over at her husband. He was sleeping on his side of the bed, snoring softly like he always did. It was never enough to wake her, thankfully. Not like Lola's ex-husband, who'd been a snorer of epic proportions. Henry hadn't bothered a single soul in the six and a half decades he'd been alive on this earth. Matter of fact, she couldn't think of a single person who disliked him—other than Mae herself, whenever he took the liberty of dipping into the brownie batter, or when he insisted on sneaking up behind her while she was cooking, nipping at the lobe of her ear, then dancing away and laughing when she tried to swat him with a spoon and inevitably sprayed chocolate batter all over the kitchen.

But the truth of the matter was that she could never bring herself to stay irked at him. It wasn't just his physical looks, although he certainly wasn't hurting in that department. The same things she'd fallen in love with at that Boston bar forty-plus years ago were still present and accounted for. The long, proud nose. Full lips, always eager to twitch into a smile. Bright blue eyes that danced in the sunlight when he laughed, cried, and—well, all the time, really. And that darn shock of hair that was perpetually threatening to fall over his forehead. She reached over and smoothed it out of his face now. Time had turned his sun-drenched blondness into something more silvery, but in Mae's eyes, he was all the more handsome for it.

But, even more than his good looks, Mae loved Henry's soul. He was a selfless giver, an instant friend to every child who'd ever come across his path. He loved nothing more than to kneel in front of an awestruck five-year-old and present him or her with some little hand-carved trinket, one of the many he kept in his pockets to whittle whenever he had an idle moment. She loved that he laughed and cried in all the wrong places during romantic comedies and that he knew how to cook—how to *really* cook, the kind of cooking you do with a jazz record crooning through the speakers and a soft breeze drifting in through an open window.

She let her hand linger on Henry's forehead just a beat too long. He didn't open his eyes, but his hand snaked up from underneath the sheets and threaded through Mae's fingers.

"You're getting up?"

"Can't waste the day away."

It was a ritual, one they'd been through practically every morning for as long as either could remember. For all that he'd become a proud father to four children, a state-record-holding fisherman, a much-sought-after contractor and builder on the island of Nantucket, Henry loved nothing so much as to stay in bed for hours, alternating between sleeping and poking Mae until she rolled over and gave him the soft kisses he called her "hummingbird pecks." There was a perpetual little boy spirit in him, a playfulness that another six or sixty decades couldn't extinguish if it tried.

"Stay with me," he murmured. "The day can wait a few more minutes, can't it?" His eyes were open now, heavy with sleep, but still gazing at her fondly.

Mae tapped him playfully on the tip of the nose. "If it was up to you, 'a few more minutes' would turn into hours before we knew it, and then I'd be scrambling around like a chicken with my head cut off, trying to get everything done before Holly, Pete, and the kids get here tonight."

Holly was Mae and Henry's middle daughter. She and her husband, Pete, were bringing their two kids to Nantucket to spend the weekend. Mae had had the date circled on her calendar for months, excited at the prospect of spoiling her grandkids rotten. She already had oodles of activities planned—walks downtown to get rock candy from the corner store, sandcastles at the beach, bike rides down to 'Sconset to ogle the grand houses the rich folks had built out on that end of the island.

Grady was a little wrecking ball of a seven-year-old boy, and Mae knew that he'd love nothing so much as building a massive sandcastle and then terrorizing it like a blond Godzilla. Alice, on the other hand, was still as sweet and loving as a five-year-old girl could be. She let Grandma Mae braid her long, soft hair into fishtails every morning whenever they were visiting the island. It was another ritual that Mae treasured beyond anything else. Her life was full of those kinds of moments.

"It ain't so bad, lying in bed with me, is it?" Henry teased. "But maybe I just won't give ya a choice!"

He leaped up and threw his arms around Mae's waist, tugging her over him and then dragging them both beneath the covers. Mae yelped in surprise and smacked him on the chest, but Henry was a big man—nearly six and a half feet tall—and the years he'd spent hauling in fish during his weekend trips with Brent had kept him muscular and toned. When her palm landed on his shoulder, it just made a thwacking noise, and did about as much good as if she'd slapped a brick wall. So she just laughed and let Henry pull her into his arms, roll over on top of her, and throw the comforter over their heads.

It was soft and warm and white underneath. The April sun filtered through the bedsheets and cast everything in a beautiful, hazy glow. "You've never looked so beautiful," Henry said, his face suspended above hers.

"Henry Benson, I do believe you are yanking my chain," she admonished.

"Never," he said, and he said it with such utter seriousness that Mae's retort fell from her lips. Instead of poking him in the chest like she always did whenever he teased her, she let her hand stroke the line of his jaw.

He pressed a gentle kiss to her lips. "Stay with me for just a few more minutes, Mrs. Benson," he said. She could feel him smiling as he kissed her. She could also feel the butterflies fluttering in her stomach. Forty-one years of marriage and four children later, and she still got butterflies when her husband kissed her. Wasn't that something?

"All right, Mr. Benson," she said, letting her head fall back on the pillows. "Just a few more minutes."

Henry grinned and fell in next to her, pulling her into his embrace. She could feel his heartbeat thumping in his chest. Familiar. Dependent. Reliable. Hers. "You just made my day."

"But I'm warning you," she continued, raising one finger into the air and biting back the smile that wanted to steal over her lips. "If you start snoring again, I'm smothering you with a pillow."

"Warning received," Henry said. "Now quit making a fuss and snooze with me for a while, darling."

So Mae did exactly that. Sara's plants could wait.

Click here to keep reading!

JOIN MY MAILING LIST!

Click the link below to join my mailing list and receive updates, freebies, release announcements, and more!

JOIN HERE:

https://sendfox.com/lp/19y8p3

ALSO BY GRACE PALMER

Sunny Isle of Palms

The Beach Baby

The Beach Date

The Beach B&B

The Wayfarer Inn

The Vineyard Sisters

The Vineyard Mothers

The Vineyard Daughters

Sweet Island Inn

No Home Like Nantucket (Book 1)

No Beach Like Nantucket (Book 2)

No Wedding Like Nantucket (Book 3)

No Love Like Nantucket (Book 4)

No Secret Like Nantucket (Book 5)

No Forever Like Nantucket (Book 6)

Willow Beach Inn

Just South of Paradise (Book 1)

Just South of Perfect (Book 2)

Just South of Sunrise (Book 3)

Just South of Christmas (Book 4)